OUT OF EDEN

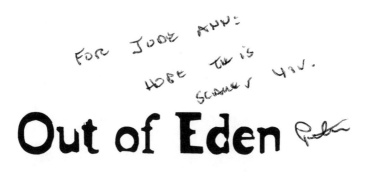

For Jude Anne
Hope this
scares you.

Out of Eden

PETER JOHNSON

namelos

South Hampton, New Hampshire

First Edition

Library of Congress Control Number: 2013931031

ISBN 978-1-60898-160-1 (hardcover : alk. paper)
ISBN 978-1-60898-161-8 (paperback : alk. paper)
ISBN 978-1-60898-162-5 (ebook)

www.namelos.com

For David Stokes and Urban Voll

Leopold couldn't shake the roar of the Falls from his head, or his fantasy of the precipice breaking loose, hundreds of tourists tumbling into the mist, their fierce screams soothing him— so lost in his daydream Abraham had to drag him from the observation platform, both of them wet and laughing, drawing stares from tourists except for her, a disheveled Asian woman going through a garbage can by the restrooms, carrying a little brown canvas bag, dressed in what looked like a night-gown, Abraham seeing her too, so now there would be trouble, because Abraham would want her, and so they took her with them in the Taurus, because that was the deal he had struck with Abraham, knowing she'd be disposed of, like the others— and the men of the city shall stone her with stones—*all this converging with the echo of the roar as they followed the Niagara River, then over a bridge into a city littered with boarded-up stores and rusty steel plants, until a normal hunger struck and they pulled into a little park, squatting under a tree, watching six men weighed down with golf bags approach a green fronted by a polluted pond, and across that, two other men standing on a brown patch of ground, holding clubs in their hands.*

"Give me the binoculars, Abraham," Leopold said, "and you"—pointing to the Asian woman at his feet—"don't say a word or you'll be sorry," Abraham laughing, taking a bite of the meatball sub he'd bought before entering the park.

Stony pulled out of the cemetery, mistakenly shifting the Forester into fourth gear. It bucked a few times, then stalled in the middle of the road. His mother, who was sitting next to him, gasped as a shiny black pickup truck, its chassis riding high above two oversize tires, squealed to a stop. The truck was so close he could see the man behind the wheel. His large head was shaved, and he had a silver ring the size of an Oreo dangling from his left ear. He was swearing, his meaty arms quivering with each obscenity. Stony's mother lowered her window and shouted, "Give it a rest, the kid just got his permit."

"Screw you, lady," he yelled.

"Let it go, Mom," Stony said. "The guy's a jerk."

By the time Stony had finished his sentence, she was out of the car. She'd been a track star in college and still ran and lifted, but she was no match for the guy in the truck. Stony eyed his golf clubs resting behind the back seat and wondered if he could lay hands on his three-iron.

When he turned around, his mother was leaning toward the window of the pickup, both hands on her hips, nose to nose with the driver. "Screw you back," she said.

The guy looked startled, then laughed. He wagged his tongue in a crude sexual way as he slowly backed up the truck before peeling away.

"Did you see what he did with his tongue?" she asked when she returned to the car. "If I ever see you do that to a girl, Stony, you'll be sorry." Before Stony could respond, cars started honking behind them. "Just pull over to the curb," she said. "Everyone's in a big hurry today."

Stony was beginning to see this mishap as another bad omen. First, a visit to the cemetery to place flowers on his grandfather's grave, then the guy with the truck, and now he had to face his biggest test: playing golf with his father, whom he hadn't seen in a month and who had planned a "family trip" to New Hampshire with Stony, his sister Molly, and Sally, his father's live-in girlfriend.

"Sorry, Mom," Stony said, maneuvering the car next to the curb, "but no one drives a standard anymore."

"That's because they're lazy like your father."

"What does Dad have to do with it?"

"Did you think I'd forget your father's old rattrap is an automatic?"

"Geez," was all Stony could say. In fact, his father's car wasn't a rattrap but a mint-condition, blue 1984 Grand Marquis with leather seats and a thousand-dollar stereo system, equipped with a special amplifier switch under the steering wheel.

His mother finally composed herself, brushing strands of brown hair from her forehead. Yesterday she had it cut short like his sister's, and she wasn't used to bangs, always touching them as if they made her forehead itch. "Sorry," she said, resting her hand on his. "You know I want you to have fun with your father."

"I know," Stony said, pulling away from the curb. In front of them was the Basilica, an old church that was so enormous and ornate it could have been transplanted from some medieval Italian city. He glanced up at the elegant white angels suspended from four large domes flanking the entrance. They were pressing marble trumpets to their lips, trying to scare off demons.

"Did I ever tell you the story about that church?" his mother asked. "How Father Baker prayed for money, and when they began construction, the excavators hit natural gas?"

"You've told me about a hundred times."

His mother ignored him. "You know, your grandmother used to give tours there after she retired."

"Yeah, I know," Stony said.

"Well, it doesn't hurt to remind you of the good things in the world. Life isn't just gloom and doom."

Stony didn't know if she was trying to convince him or herself, since she, like him, was still haunted by his grandmother's violent death, even though it had happened six years before. Visiting his grandfather's grave made it impossible not to think about it.

When they reached the Basilica, he made a left toward a glass-domed building that housed the Botanical Gardens, finally gliding into the parking lot of a golf course. His father was waiting for them next to the first tee, leaning against a red ball-washer and talking to some old guys. A stranger would have said he looked like a movie star—tall, blond, and athletic, with high cheekbones and a small nose. His jaw was square and strong, his chin dimpled by a slight cleft. He was wearing a snug white T-shirt with writing on it that Stony couldn't decipher.

As he approached the car, Stony's mother said, "Oh no, what does he want now?"

"Let's not have any trouble," Stony pleaded.

"Just grab your clubs before he revs up his engine."

But it was too late. His father had already stationed himself near the passenger door and was helping Stony's mother out of the car. "Nice wheels, Kate. You've finally sold out and bought an SUV."

"It's not an SUV," his mother explained. "It has four cylinders and the same chassis as an Outback."

"Looks like an SUV to me," his father said, smiling. "Another gas guzzler to fill the pockets of white-collar creeps."

"Oh, give me a break," his mother said. "Nice T-shirt, too."

Stony could now read the green print on his father's chest: SOUTH BUFFALO BOYS DO IT BETTER.

"At least they got the 'boys' right," his mother said.

"Geez." Stony sighed and got out of the car. He grabbed his golf bag from the back and tried to escape into the clubhouse.

"Can't you see you're embarrassing Stony?" his father said.

She laughed again and pushed his father aside as she circled the car. She jumped into the driver's seat, started the engine, and began to pull away. "Goodbye, sweetie," she said.

"Goodbye, sweetie," Stony's father replied, trailing behind the moving car. "And I like your hair. You look like a little gymnast."

Stony stood there, feeling the weight of the golf bag on his shoulder. "I think she was talking to me."

"Just having fun, Stony. What's her problem?"

"We went to Grandpa's grave, then almost had an accident."

"Why did you go to his grave?"

"It's his birthday."

His father grimaced. "Stony," he said, "with all due respect for the dead, your grandfather was the man who destroyed my marriage. One day your mother realized she didn't marry her father, and it was downhill from there. And I'll never forgive him for how he fell apart after your grandmother's murder. Your mother really needed him then."

Stony had heard this complaint before, so he didn't respond, but he was surprised by his father's use of the word "murder." Usually people said things like "passed" or "unexpectedly taken away."

"I could tell you stories, Stony," his father added, but fortunately he decided not to. Instead, he grabbed Stony playfully by the arm and said, "God, you look great."

That was his father in a nutshell. Stony hadn't seen him in a month, but with a phrase or two, or a squeeze of an arm, Stony was five years old again, following him around the house like a poodle.

"Let me take your bag," his father said, grabbing it. They began walking toward the clubhouse. "We don't tee off for forty-five minutes, so let's get a Coke. Myron's looking forward to seeing you."

Inside, his father stopped by tables and bragged about Stony's prowess on the baseball field, even though he hadn't been to a game that spring, or praised Stony's grades, even though he hadn't been to a teacher's conference or seen a report card. But Stony still loved to hear him talk, loved to watch his body language and see his infectious smile. He could work a room as gracefully as a politician, and the men in the clubhouse respected him.

Lately Stony hadn't played at South Park, going instead to private clubs where his friends belonged, so he almost laughed when over the entrance to the clubhouse he saw a long, green ten-foot-by-eight-inch wooden sign with SOUTH PARK COUNTRY CLUB painted in large white letters. It was a short nine-hole course, with dirt instead of grass tees. And the holes were far from picturesque, arranged around a stagnant pond spotted with rust-colored lily pads. To make things worse, the entire course was encircled by an asphalt road, where teenagers raced their sports cars.

But in spite of its shortcomings, Stony had a soft spot for the course. This was where he'd learned to play golf. He also had good memories of the clubhouse, with its heavy wooden tables and creaking chairs. When he was a kid, his father would drop him and a few friends off on summer days at 7 a.m. and pick them up at 3 p.m. They'd play thirty-six holes and sip Cokes while eating peanut butter or tuna fish sandwiches their mothers had packed. And Myron still worked the bar and grill, which was where Stony and his father ended up after making the rounds of three tables.

Myron was an overweight ex-railroad guy with a cherubic face and one leg; he'd lost the other under a wheel of a railroad car. He always wore tight white T-shirts and blue painter's pants with one leg rolled up and secured with a safety pin. He refused to get an artificial leg, taking pride in how he maneuvered around the bar on one crutch. He compensated for the lost leg by lifting weights he kept in the back room. His chest was enormous, his biceps as large as Stony's thighs.

"Arthur and son," Myron said with a laugh, when they sat down. He poured two Cokes, then scanned a sheet listing tee times. "Listen up," he shouted to tables of men finishing off hot dogs and mugs of cold beer. "Art's teeing off after Al Capone." Everyone laughed, including Stony's father.

"Did your dad tell you about Al Capone?" Myron asked, shaking his head.

"You mean the gangster?"

Now everyone was laughing.

"He wishes," Myron said. "The guy's a punk crackhead from Lackawanna who hangs with a bunch of wannabe gangsta boys. But your dad put him straight."

Stony thought about the many times his father had "put someone straight." One summer the heel from one of Stony's sister's shoes broke off, and when the shoe store wouldn't exchange them, Stony's father dragged him down to the mall, where he pinned the store manager against a display window until security guards arrived. Stony could only imagine what Al Capone had done to incite his father's wrath.

Myron was about to continue when a little bell rang. At the sound he hobbled over to a toaster oven and removed a hot ham and cheese sandwich, which one of the men sitting at the tables came over to fetch. While this was happening, six guys—strangers to Stony—stumbled through the clubhouse's screen door. Stony tracked everyone's reaction, noticing that the mood had suddenly darkened. Half-shaved and dressed in what appeared to be secondhand polo shirts, faded jeans, and beat-up tennis shoes, they didn't look too dangerous, except for one guy who had to be the one they called Al Capone. He was squat and powerfully built, as if he spent most of his time at the gym. He had heavily greased wavy black hair, chiseled features, a dark complexion, and a short beard spread unevenly on his face. He wore a red, flower-print shirt tucked into the beltless waistband of shiny gray pants. The pants themselves had uncuffed bottoms falling a few inches short of a new pair of white alligator golf shoes. To Stony, he looked like a pimp, or maybe he was just a bad dresser. He walked over to the bar, ignoring Stony and his father, while his friends positioned themselves near the door.

"Two threesomes," he said to Myron, laying down some cash on the bar. Myron took the money, shaking his head and mumbling to himself as he opened the cash register. He deposited the green fees and returned with a handful of scorecards.

"Remember," he said, "everyone uses their own clubs." Then he tapped the side of the man's head with the tip of a pencil. "Got it?"

When Myron poked the man, an expression flashed over his face that made Stony catch his breath. "I got it," he said, grabbing the scorecards and heading over to his friends, who were still standing expressionless by the door. Finally they all left, occasionally glancing behind them.

"Did you see the look he gave me," Myron said. "I noticed he didn't give *you* that look, Art."

Myron turned to Stony. "Last week that idiot scraped your father's car with his pull cart and tried to walk away, thinking no one saw him." Myron started to laugh. "Next thing I see is your old man chasing down this old black Altima."

Stony's father laughed loudly, shrugging his shoulders in mock confusion. "What could I do?"

After Myron finished giving details of the encounter, Stony and his father spent the next ten minutes drinking their Cokes and listening to Myron's theories on everything from aliens to midgets, the latter a group for whom he had great sympathy. Then they paid for their Cokes and went to the first tee. His father sat on a yellow metal bench and said, "Don't end up a punk like that jerk in the clubhouse."

"He didn't seem so scary," Stony said, though in fact there *was* something spooky about the guy.

"Well, he's been arrested a few times for beating on his wife, and it's common knowledge he deals drugs to kids. You know how I feel about that stuff."

"Where did you hear that?" Stony asked, knowing his father had a penchant for exaggerating.

"Ah, so you're one of those benefit-of-the-doubt kind of guys?" his father said.

Stony didn't like where this conversation was heading, so he didn't answer. Instead, he looked down the fairway at one of the threesomes, anxious to get started. His father got up and walked toward the tee, then said, "Let the morons finish up before we hit. That way we won't have to slow down." Stony agreed, and they both sat down on the bench.

As they waited, his father seemed to forget about the man with the beard. "Let's play for a dollar a hole," he said to Stony. "Isn't that what the guys at the country club do?"

Stony had been hoping the conversation wouldn't turn this way—comments about his friends' private clubs, about rich girls Stony was no doubt dating (he wished!), and about a wager. His father was not only a bad golfer but a notoriously bad loser.

"Let's just play for fun," Stony said.

"What are you afraid of?" His father walked over to his bag, withdrew his driver, and thrust it forward like a sword. He grabbed its club face and jabbed the grip into Stony's side. "*En garde*," he teased.

Stony felt an old anger rise up in him. He dodged one of the thrusts, then smiled and said, "Let's make it two dollars."

"That's my boy," his father crooned.

After Stony made the bet, he felt like crying. He knew he'd win because his father was an even worse golfer under pressure.

"You go first," his father said.

The first hole was a short par four with a narrow fairway, guarded on the left by the road and on the right by a number of huge oak trees. Stony teed up and scanned the fairway, noticing the second threesome walking off the green.

"Don't drive into those trees, now," his father joked.

Stony swung and hit a beautiful high draw that carried the trees and landed in the middle of the fairway about sixty yards from the green.

"Big deal," his father said. "You have a lousy short game, anyway."

Stony didn't say a word, didn't even smile. He stood next to the tee as his father readied himself, wiggling his driver back and forth. His father took a vicious swing and almost fell down as his ball sliced toward the trees.

Stony nearly laughed but then felt bad. "There's a lot of room there, Dad," he said. "You'll probably have a shot to the green."

His father calmly returned the driver to the bag. "I don't need your cheerleading," he said. "We're not at the country club, okay?"

"Yeah, sure," Stony said, thinking, *And now it begins.* They walked down the fairway, Stony trying to make small talk, but his father was fixed on the trees. When they got there, they found his ball. It was a good lie, but to reach the green he'd have to thread a shot through a five-foot opening between two thick tree trunks.

"I'd probably drop from there," Stony said. "I won't count the stroke and you can give me one later."

"Spare me," his father said, removing a five-iron from his bag. Stony sought protection behind a tree as his father addressed the ball and let it rip. The ball hit one tree on the left, careened into the trunk of another on the right, and, much to Stony's astonishment, shot out onto the fairway. From there his father hit an eight-iron a few feet to the left of the green.

For Stony's second shot, he hit a soft wedge about five feet from the pin.

"You still have to make the putt," his father said, trying to unnerve him, but Stony calmly putted in for a birdie after his father had chipped onto the green and one-putted for a five.

"The important thing," his father said, "is that I didn't quit. I made you play your best. It's not just about the money."

Instead of replying, Stony headed toward the second tee, followed by his father. On the way there, they passed Al Capone and his crew, who were tracking their balls on the fairway. For some reason they had decided to play together.

Stony's father confronted their leader. "You can't play with six guys," he said.

"It's not six guys," the man said, smiling, "it's two threesomes."

"Well, we're driving into you," Stony's father yelled, hurrying to the next tee.

Once they got there, Stony saw in the distance Al Capone and his friends picking up their balls and throwing them close to the green. Meanwhile, Stony's father ripped his driver from his bag and probed his front pocket for a tee. The ground was packed solid, so when he pushed the tee into the dirt, it broke. "Damn," he said. Finally he got one to stick.

The fairway of the second hole, flanked on both sides by a hundred yards of big oaks, was treacherous, but Stony's father hit one of the straightest and longest drives of his life. The ball nearly reached the sixsome, one of whom turned and waved back, making his father even angrier. And this was how he played the hole—in a rush, but with a cool single-mindedness that raised the level of play. His father's only disappointment came when they reached the third tee and discovered that Al Capone had already teed off.

The third hole was intimidating. Between the tee and the green was a hundred and fifty yards of water, and if you carried it, you still had to deal with a twenty-yard-wide sand trap in front of the green and an asphalt road behind it. Stony had rarely seen his father make it over the pond on the first try.

When they reached the tee, the sixsome was chipping onto the green from various places. Stony's father emptied the balls from his bag, looking frustrated that he only had five. He asked Stony for more, so Stony handed him about ten shiny Titleists. "Idiots," Stony's father said, teeing up one after another.

His first shot arced high over the pond and landed in the middle of the green. Stony could see Al Capone flinch as the ball fell a few feet from him. The next shot faded in from the left, making one of the other golfers lose his balance and tumble into a sand trap. "Yes!" Stony's father yelled.

Even when he hit a low liner, it skipped the last twenty yards of the pond and nearly hit another guy in the leg. With each shot the men scattered in different directions, until Al Capone decided to grab a ball and hurl it into the pond, shaking his fist at Stony's father. The other men followed his lead, and so it went for a good three or four minutes: Stony's father hitting balls with his eight-iron, the men tossing them into the water.

When he had exhausted the supply of balls, his father smiled and said, "Did you see what those guys did, Stony? They threw our balls into the water. I think we should do something about that."

With a sick feeling in his stomach, Stony followed his father through a wooded path that led to the green. By the time they got there, all six men had claimed it, crouched around the pin, brandishing their putters. As Stony watched, his father reached for his driver and leaped onto the green, momentarily scattering the men. When they surrounded him, he waved his driver in circles to keep them at bay. "Get help," his father yelled.

Stony ran toward the clubhouse, which was a half mile down the road, wondering what Myron or any of those old guys could do. On the way there, he heard laughter coming from two sleazy-looking guys perched on the hood of a brown station wagon, which itself was parked under a tree behind the green. They were obviously enjoying his father's antics, and Stony felt like yelling at them. But then he noticed his father's Grand Marquis in the parking lot and remembered the extra key hidden in the glove compartment and the foot-long metal pipe under the seat. He ran toward the car, looking behind him as his father continued to swing the club in a wide arc, laughing like a lunatic.

When Stony reached the car, he found the key and started the engine, Jimi Hendrix's primal yawp blasting from the cassette player. The song was "Voodoo Child," and Stony listened to the lyrics, pulling out of the parking lot and gunning the engine once, twice. As he approached the fourth green, his father smiled, glad the cavalry had finally arrived.

Stony knew what the program called for: he was to drive up to the green and scare the hell out of Al Capone and his buddies. If necessary, he could toss his father the pipe and see if they might back down. But as he watched his father hold off the angry sixsome, he decided that this time things would be different. He reached under the steering column and clicked on the amplifier switch, feeling the whole car trembling with Hendrix's guitar. Then he gunned the engine again, speeding past the green. At first his father seemed startled, but then his eyes locked onto Stony's and he smiled, as if enjoying the decision Stony had just made. Stunned and angered by that smile, Stony drove even faster, watching his father disappear in the rearview mirror. His hands began to shake, so he gripped the steering wheel tighter, listening to Hendrix chant, *'cause I'm a voodoo child, God knows, I'm a voodoo child, baby.*

After a few minutes the two across the water came into focus, a tall blond man and a boy, the blond man smiling, toying with golf balls, rolling them back forth on the ground like huge white marbles, as the boy looked on, shaking his head, Leopold then shifting the binoculars to the six men on the green only a hundred feet away, focusing on a bearded man wearing shiny white shoes that Leopold wanted, the way he had wanted that cowboy hat with the snakeskin band from the man in Iowa who the police thought had hanged himself, the thought making him smile, and Leopold would've gladly had a go at the bearded man, but he, like his friends, was preoccupied with golf balls raining down on them, while the two across the pond disappeared from sight, only to arrive a few minutes later, the blond man waving a metal club at the other six while the boy drifted toward the road, looking in the direction of a large building about a hundred yards away.

"Damn," Abraham said, his mouth half full of meatballs, "what kind of crazy is this?"

Leopold not answering but knowing his next victim

was among them, a thought like a heaviness now instead of a fire, because he couldn't stop the killing any more than he would be able to keep from handcuffing the Asian woman to the car at nightfall, but feeling sure this time it was the man with the shiny white shoes, though also drawn to the blond man on the green, who looked like one of those perfect models on the magazine covers he had spied as a boy at the local convenience store—a memory making him angry, as he watched the blond man hold off the other six while the boy jogged toward the building down the road, then broke into a run right past Leopold and Abraham, Leopold thinking, No, it's him, the boy, but why?

"Damn," *Abraham said, doing a little jig.* "That's some kind of crazy."

"Now, now," *Leopold said, smiling,* "be calm and a plan shall reveal itself."

Stony was holed up in his room when his mother tapped on the door.

"I know you're in there," she said.

He didn't answer. He'd been comatose on his bed for what seemed like an hour, still holding the keys to his father's car.

"You better come out," he heard Molly say. "The jig's up, you're going over the Falls in a cellophane barrel. You're disappearing in the mist." He could picture her smiling, and he wanted to remind her how embarrassed she was when their father nearly strangled that shoe salesman at the mall.

"This isn't funny, Molly," his mother said, though she was laughing too. "Really, Stony," she added. "Your father wasn't even mad. He just wants his car back."

Stony went to the door, placing his ear to the

cool wood, hoping to hear them walk away. When he cracked it open, he was confronted by their faces, no more than a foot from his own.

"Come out, sweetie," his mother pleaded.

"Boy, are you in trouble," his sister said. She had a round face, a tiny nose, and large, startling blue eyes. Her red hair was short and cut into bangs, and just recently, at fifteen, she'd moved out of girlhood and had become beautiful. It bothered Stony when he saw his friends gawking at her. But he didn't feel very brotherly now. She was being a wise guy, enjoying his situation.

"This is very bad timing," she said, waving her finger at him, "especially with the trip just two weeks away."

"Downstairs, Molly," her mother ordered.

As she left, Molly said Stony should be thinking of a good place to escape to. "Somewhere exotic," she said, "like Cancún or Costa Rica. They like Americans there."

"Downstairs," her mother repeated.

When she left, Stony opened the door and returned to his bed. His mother joined him. He could smell her perfume, and her closeness made him uncomfortable.

"What did he do this time?" she asked.

"You mean he didn't tell you?"

"He just said you had his car and he wanted it back."

Stony told her most of the story, leaving out only his father's comment about his grandfather, since if she heard it she'd get defensive and rehash every dirty detail of the divorce. She laughed at moments in the story when his father had acted most like an idiot, which didn't surprise him. If she had been there, she probably would've been at his father's side, poking a club into Al Capone's ribs.

His parents had gotten divorced because his father had been unfaithful, but they still had a weird connection. It wouldn't have surprised Stony if they met periodically in a motel behind Sally's back, the woman his father was currently living with, except that it would have made his mother as dishonest as the women his father had cheated with. And that's what had sent her over the edge, discovering that everyone, except her, had known about the affairs, until Mrs. Corbett, a retiree from across the street, told her about one particular woman his father had brought home at lunchtime.

His mother couldn't forgive that kind of humiliation, and she often made Stony and Molly aware of it. Many times Stony had wanted to ask his father how he could've have acted so despicably. He had even rehearsed a speech that ended with "How would you feel if I cheated on a girl?"

Stony's mother began to massage his neck, making him even more uncomfortable.

"He's really not mad?" Stony asked.

"He just wants his car back."

"Weird."

Stony's mother stood and faced him. "Not weird at all. It's pretty routine by now. Whatever was bugging him is out of his system and he can relax for a few days. He seemed more amused than anything. Just bring the car back and I'll follow you. You can drop it off and leave the keys in the ignition, then run to my car and we can speed off like two vandals."

"I can't legally drive by myself," Stony reminded her.

"It's just a couple of blocks, and you seemed fine making it home from the golf course." She was smiling.

"What's so funny?" he asked.

"When you spend more time with your father, you might understand."

Stony thought that doubtful. He planned to go to college far away from Buffalo, but first he had to face his father.

It was a short drive to the working-class neighborhood where his father lived in a small, boxy house that he had inherited from his own father, whose death coincided with Stony's parents' divorce. At first it was depressing for Stony to visit his father there. He seemed a bit lost, unable to make himself dinner or clean the house, which was strewn with ketchup-stained wrappers from fast-food joints. But then he met Sally and the house didn't smell like old people anymore. All the knickknacks and framed pictures of the Pope were replaced by scented candles and paintings of sunsets and mountains, and the living room furniture, previously preserved in form-fitting plastic, gave way to a leather recliner and couch. A lot of people had moved out of the neighborhood, but Stony's father loved to describe how his own father's generation worked swing shifts dressed in blue or gray khaki pants and shirts, carrying black lunchboxes filled with bologna sandwiches and thermoses of hot coffee.

Stony's mother was driving so close behind him that he could see her smiling, as if happily anticipating another confrontation with his father, though she had promised not to interfere.

As Stony steered the car into the driveway and slowed to a stop, he could see his father and Sally sitting on the front porch, his father holding a beer and Sally tossing a tennis ball from hand to hand. His mother pulled into the driveway behind him and, ignoring her promise, stepped out of her car. Stony sighed.

When he turned off the engine, his father moved quickly toward him, smiling, as if nothing had happened. He even opened Stony's door and helped him out. "I didn't think you had it in you," his father said. He was wearing a different tight white T-shirt, this one with a huge black question mark on it. "You look surprised I'm in one piece. You're probably thinking: did he fight those nasty guys or run away?"

Stony knew running away was never a possibility for his father. But he did wonder what had happened, so he asked, "Are you okay?"

His father did a pirouette, which made even his mother laugh. "Your running away saved me, Stony."

"What?"

"When you drove by and I saw that look on your face"—he tried to mimic it, bugging his eyes out as if someone had kicked him in the groin—"I couldn't stop laughing. I fell to my knees and rolled around on the green. Those guys just froze. They thought I was crazy."

"I think they were on to something," Stony's mother said, eliciting a laugh from Sally.

His father ignored them. "At any rate, when I got up, I leaned your bag against a tree and warned them not to touch it, and I played through. I played really well."

"I bet you did," Stony's mother said, leaning back against the hood of her car.

Sally laughed again.

"Hi, Sally," his mother said.

"Hi, Kate. Sorry about this." Unlike Stony's family, Sally wasn't hardwired with anxiety. She was an avid hiker, short but very strong. She had a small, pretty face, gray eyes, and a thin, delicate neck that, along with her perfect posture, made her appear sophisticated. Her long brown hair was tied into a ponytail, and she was wearing a red T-shirt, hiking shorts, and running shoes.

Even Stony's mother liked Sally. At first this surprised him, but then he realized Sally had appeared a year after the divorce, so there was no reason to hate her, especially since she seemed to stabilize his father. Also, Sally was a counselor at a local high school, and Stony's mother, who was a middle-school teacher, admired that.

"He's your problem now, not mine," his mother said.

"Tell me about it," Sally replied.

"Won't anyone take up my cause?" his father pleaded. "You're not going to desert me twice in one day, are you, Stony?"

Stony handed him the keys and started toward his mother's car.

"That's enough drama for one day," Sally said, dragging his father toward the porch, then doubling back to Stony. "You know, he didn't mean to get you upset."

"He never means it," Stony's mother protested, and Sally shrugged again, explaining that his father was still a "work in progress."

"Been there, done that," his mother said.

"Can we just leave?" Stony asked.

"What are you all saying about me?" his father yelled from the porch, grabbing the beer and taking a swig.

Stony almost screamed, "That you're an idiot," but he couldn't muster up that level of courage.

Sally touched Stony's arm before he walked away. "Will you and your sister visit a few times before the trip? I think it might be good to establish some kind of rhythm."

Stony nodded, then got into his mother's car. As they drove away, he waved lamely to his father.

"Cheer up," his father yelled. "In two weeks, nothing but kayaking and fishing and golf."

Stony liked kayaking and fishing and golf, but right now he would have preferred living in the Gulag, spearing fishheads with a rusty fork from a clay bowl of cold potato soup. Still, he forced a smile as he and his mother drove away. "You sure you don't have trouble with this trip?" he asked.

"Of course not. In fact, I'd rather you go with her than him."

"I was thinking you might be concerned about him messing up my head."

His mother looked perplexed, as if she'd never thought about that possibility. "That's a little dramatic, isn't it?" she said. "It's only a week."

Only a week, Stony thought.

Molly was waiting for him and his mother when they got home. She was lying on the couch, a book in one hand, a half-eaten tomato in the other, pink juice glistening on the bridge of flesh spanning her upper lip.

"Don't stain my new couch, Molly," his mother said.

Molly licked away the juice, resting her book on the hardwood floor. "What's the verdict?"

His mother laughed.

"Just let it go," Stony said.

"Did he want to arm-wrestle you? Did he cancel the trip?"

Stony walked past her and up the stairs to his room.

"You can't hide, Stony. None of us can. Remember what I said about Costa Rica." Her laughter was the last thing he heard before closing his bedroom door.

When Stony went to college he wouldn't pine for his mother or father, but he'd miss Molly. Right now she was being a jerk, but she often made him laugh. That's how she dealt with problems, while Stony would go for a run or disappear into his computer. He wasn't big into video games, but he liked to Google major cities and download pictures of places he wished he could visit. He would research what the inhabitants ate or drank, what their flag looked like, and how to say hi and goodbye in their language. He would then imagine scenarios where he was studying abroad and would meet an exotic girl who would be more experienced in sex than he was, which wouldn't have been hard. Girls seemed to like him, and a few even called the house, but he had never stuck with anyone.

But he had his books. Not many novels, though he'd bought everything written by Hemingway and Flannery O'Connor. He especially liked O'Connor's characters because they seemed hopelessly damaged but had the possibility to change. Still, unlike Molly, who read nothing but old, fat, nineteenth-century novels, he didn't see much value in inventing make-believe characters when there were so many interesting living and dead real people. That's why most of his books were biographies and autobiographies, not of prestigious men and women but of oddballs or people considered to be dangerous or evil, like John Wilkes Booth or Rasputin.

Better than anyone else, he knew his need to understand a certain kind of human cruelty was a response to his grandmother's death. She was a tall, beautiful woman with fierce blue eyes and wild salt-and-pepper curls that spilled over her shoulders. Because she'd been a nurse before retiring, she owned a stethoscope, and one summer afternoon she and Stony had listened to each other's hearts. At first it scared him, but after a while he enjoyed moving the little metal cup from his chest to hers, their heartbeats engaged in a special private conversation. Sensing his initial fear, she had hugged him, saying, "Don't be afraid. There's a certainty in that beating, a kind of strength. It's who you are, and that 'who' will do great things someday."

He'd always assumed she'd be alive to help him discover that "who," but when he was eleven something terrible happened. He remembered being picked up from school early by his aunt. When they arrived home, vans from local TV stations were prowling up and down the street, his father yelling at reporters to leave them alone. He also noticed his grandfather, his mother's father, peeking out from a corner of the picture window, as if he were ashamed of something. Everything afterward was extremely fuzzy, though Stony was able to piece together the tragedy from overhearing conversations.

His grandparents had a handyman named John, whom his grandmother had met one Saturday while distributing clothes at a soup kitchen sponsored by her church. John, a Vietnam vet, was a big man with a large belly and a white beard. He always wore jeans, work boots, and plaid flannel shirts, even in the summer. When he walked he moved from side to side, ape-like, but he was a gentle man and often played catch with Stony. He was missing some teeth on top, and the remaining ones were different shades of dark yellow or brown because he smoked and chewed tobacco. But his eyes, a bright blue, were soft and kind. John didn't live with Stony's grandparents, but they were fond of him, so they'd invite him to family cookouts.

Then something went wrong. One day after cutting the lawn, John inexplicably stabbed Stony's grandmother to death, then called the police. When the police arrived, John rushed them, brandishing the knife, and they shot him dead on his grandparents' front lawn.

Stony's grades plummeted a few months later, so his mother took him to a psychologist. Off and on for the next year, he, his mother, and the therapist dissected the murder, trying to piece together the weeks before it happened, looking for signs, talking about chemical imbalances and how the horrors of Vietnam could change a man. In the end, the therapist concluded it was all "a terrible tragedy." Whether we like it or not, he said, life is "messy and sometimes inexplicable." When he said that, Stony thought, *That's it? That's the best you can do?*

For months he stumbled around feeling as if a huge iceberg were lodged in his chest, his skin sensitive, like the nerves beneath had been rubbed raw with steel wool. But gradually the horror dissipated, morphing into numbness, so that he was able to function better, get good grades, play sports, talk to people. Still, he knew he could never accept that his grandmother's death was inexplicable, so he began to read books that might explain why people do unprovoked crazy things—biographies, even a collection of essays on evil by famous philosophers, who couldn't give definitive reasons for random cruelty, but at least they tried harder than his mother's therapist. One of the things he learned, though, was that if he read too much on this topic he actually felt worse, experiencing a rage every bit as dark as the one that probably haunted John. It made him wonder if evil could go viral, which would account for Nazi Germany. Stony had already bought two biographies for the trip: one about John F. Kennedy, another about Lee Harvey Oswald.

"Don't you think that's a little weird?" Molly had said when she saw them.

"I want to see if there was a reason they crossed paths."

"You know how Dad feels about the Kennedys."

"So he should be glad I'm reading about JFK."

"But not Osgood."

"It's Oswald."

"Who cares, it was so long ago."

Stony just shook his head.

As he walked around his bedroom now, he could hear Molly and his mother talking downstairs. He spread the curtains of his bedroom window and looked down on a patch of tall sunflowers he had planted in the spring. A squadron of tiny winged insects swarmed relentlessly above the flowers' long stems, which seemed to be genuflecting toward the west, where the sun was about to set. Although it was very quiet, he felt edgy. He thought about going for a run, but he'd been outside enough for one day. He looked at his weights scattered in the corner; they had been a gift from his father last Christmas. He sat down on the bench and grabbed two thirty-pound dumbbells, doing a few bench presses, feeling the blood rush to his arms and chest. It felt good, so he kept the weight low and did twenty repetitions, wondering how strong he could get before the New Hampshire vacation.

When he'd finished his workout he took a shower, threw on some pajama bottoms, and lay on the bed. There was a light knock, followed by his mother's voice. "Can we talk, Stony?"

"Can't it wait till tomorrow?"

"But I have something for you." She opened the door and came in.

He went to his dresser and put on a T-shirt before sitting on the bed, where his mother joined him. She was cradling a little white box in her palm.

"I wasn't going to give you this until your eighteenth birthday, but it's a good time now, and if it doesn't fit, we can have it sized before you go away."

"Sized?"

When she opened the box, Stony saw the ring his grandfather had found years before while cleaning out a railroad car at the steel plant. It was a large, square tiger's-eye ring, the stone carved into the image of a conquistador. Actually, two conquistadors—one smaller profile laid over a larger one. Before Stony's mother gave the ring to his father, she'd had it polished and had researched the gemstone, discovering that many people believed tiger's eye was beneficial for spiritual health and for achieving clarity. His father thought all of this was mumbo-jumbo, and at first refused to wear the ring because it was a gift from her father. He argued, only half jokingly, that it was cursed in some way. But then one day he slid it on, and it received so much attention that he continued to wear it—that is, until the night he and Stony's mother split up. After their argument, he removed the ring, blessed it, laughed, and tossed it into the field behind their house, saying he had finally exor-

cised the "demon," meaning his father-in-law. Stony still
remembered that night—how his father tugged on the
ring, fighting to slide it off his finger, then grabbed some
WD-40 from the garage and squirted oil around the
band until it came off. Stony and his mother spent half
the next day with a weed whacker until they found it.

Considering this history, Stony wondered whether
it was a particularly good idea to wear the ring, but he,
too, felt, as his father once did, that it was one very cool
ring. "You really want me to have this?" he asked his
mother.

"As long as you think about your grandfather
when you wear it."

"But it has a lot of bad vibes."

"If you want, we can take it to the Basilica and dip
it in holy water."

Stony laughed as he removed it from the box. He
slid it onto the ring finger of his right hand and was surprised when it fit perfectly.

*Normally, it was easy to hide and wait—an unlocked summer
cottage, a deserted dirt road running into nothing but overgrowth,
even an abandoned factory, though there you had to beat off rats,
or stare them down if you wanted to have fun, but here, just small
houses, people walking or jogging, men moving in and out of jobs
at odd hours, too easy to draw attention, so once they followed the
boy out of the park, once they located his house, they kept on the
move, staying in the park by day and driving into the country at
night, waiting for the boy to lead them to the blond man, because
now he knew the blond man and the boy were next, the Asian
woman just a diversion, so he'd let Abraham have his fun as long
as she didn't act up, but no, it wasn't her, it was the man and the
boy, the inevitability of their fate persisting, like the memory of*

*an old beating, or maybe luck—no, not luck, but necessity, that
brought Leopold and Abraham there in the early morning when
the blond man and his woman, so pretty,* like Jezebel who
thought herself a prophetess, *pulled up to the boy's house,
then later left with him and a girl, Leopold telling Abraham to
stay back, hidden behind a parked pickup truck, while he focused
the binoculars, nothing left but to follow the hunger, an ache
keeping him alive in spite of, no, because of, its horror.*

Stony and Molly sat quietly on the front porch. He'd
been awake most of the night with a nervous stomach,
so he wasn't interested in eating the blueberry pancakes
his mother had made for breakfast. Molly looked worse,
like she was awaiting execution, fidgeting with a cuff
bracelet her mother had given her the night before. It
was silver, about two inches wide, studded with three
lapis lazuli stones the size of peas. Molly had cried with
happiness after opening the gift box, but now she sat
stiffly in a white plastic lounge chair, pulling at the
bracelet and flipping through the pages of a magazine.

"Will you stop that?" Stony said.

"Stop what?"

"Turning the pages. You're not even reading the
magazine."

"Why do you care?"

"You're worried, aren't you?"

"Why should I be worried?"

"It's nothing to be ashamed of."

"It's just that this whole thing is weird," she said.
"We don't see him much, then all of a sudden we're
together for a week. How long is the drive to New
Hampshire?"

"About ten or eleven hours."

"You sure the condo's going to be big enough to get away from him?"

"Ha, so you *are* nervous. Does it have anything to do with Sally?"

Molly tossed the magazine onto a nearby beanbag chair. "No, it's him. He's crazy, and he's going to start right away with that 'Princess' stuff."

Stony laughed. "You've always been able to hold your own."

"But it's not fun. It's not easy." Her eyes widened and Stony noticed she had painted her eyelashes with mascara.

"Is that why you're wearing makeup?"

"What does that have to do with anything?"

"It's like you're dressing up for him, and it's only seven o'clock in the morning."

Molly pointed to Stony's clubs. "At least I wasn't up polishing those stupid things all night. Didn't I see you scrubbing them with a toothbrush?"

Stony laughed again, which seemed to loosen the knot in his stomach. Molly laughed too, and Stony leaned over to shake her hand. "Let's stick together on this trip, Princess. It's us against him."

"Okay, but I'm not going to let him call me Princess. Or you either."

As they were shaking on it, Stony's mother appeared on the porch in a short, light blue bathrobe. She handed him a banana and Stony thanked her.

"Is that what you're going to be wearing when they get here?" he asked.

His mother laughed loudly. "Sorry, Stony, but sometimes you sound like an old man. If it makes you uncomfortable, I'll throw on some shorts and a T-shirt." She went back into the house.

Molly was about to say something when Sally's white Toyota Highlander pulled into the driveway and gave a few short honks. They had decided to take the SUV because it would fit all four of them, plus the luggage and golf clubs.

Stony's father leaped from the driver's seat. He wore plaid madras shorts, a gray T-shirt, sport sandals, and a white painter's cap turned backward on his head. He looked wide awake, happy. Stony and Molly opened the screen door and headed toward the Highlander. When they got there his father reached out to shake his hand, and Stony wondered whether he'd feel the ring in his grip, but he didn't say a word about it. Instead, he patted Stony on the back and squeezed his bicep.

"I see you've been working out."

"He said he's going to knock you out if you act up," Molly said, which made Sally laugh.

"Princess," he said, giving her a hug, "you know me better than that." Molly grimaced, gawking at Stony as if to say, *I told you so.*

"Can we drop the 'Princess' for this trip," she said. "I'm fifteen years old."

"If that's what you want, Princess."

"Oh, no," she said.

"Come on, Stony, let's get this stuff into the car," his father said, anxiously peeking inside the house. "Where's the dragon queen?"

"Arthur," Sally said, trying to silence him.

"Just hoping to relieve the tension."

Stony helped his father with the luggage and golf clubs. The back of the Highlander was nearly full. In one corner Stony noticed some unwrapped summer toys: a black Frisbee, a Whiffle bat and ball, and a regulation-size Nerf football. At least his father was trying.

When he returned to the porch, his mother was speaking with Sally.

"Hi, Kate," his father said, interrupting, but she ignored him and continued her conversation.

"The sooner the better," his father said, clapping his hands, encouraging everyone to get into the car.

"Just let the dragon queen finish her sentence," his mother said.

"You have good ears," his father joked.

"No, you have a big mouth."

Sally looked uncomfortable, and Molly said, "Time to go."

Stony and Molly kissed their mother, and after taking his place in the back seat, Stony waved to her.

"Make sure they phone," she called to Sally.

"Don't worry, I will."

Stony's father backed out of the driveway, saying to Sally, "Aren't you two a pair of soul sisters." Then he sped away, yelling, "Yippee!" The last person Stony saw was a bathrobed Mrs. Corbett, retrieving the morning paper from her front porch. She glared at Stony's father and shook her head. Undaunted, he waved back and said, loud enough so she could hear, "You old hag."

For the first few hours of the drive, the banana Stony ate seemed to be lodged in the middle of his chest. He was sweating, his scalp itched, and he felt short of breath until he opened a window.

"It's probably best to keep the window closed," Sally said, "so the air conditioning isn't wasted."

She was right because it was already eighty degrees, but his father said, "That's okay. On this trip, Stony can do whatever he wants."

Which made Stony want to close the window.

The plan was to take the Thruway to the Mass Pike, then pick up I-495 to I-93, which would take them to New Hampshire. His father had rented a condo for a week in Ashland, about forty-five minutes north of Concord.

Two hours into the drive, Stony began to relax, mostly because of Sally, who asked him and Molly a lot of questions. Every once in a while his father would pretend to show interest, but most of the time he complained about the junk on the radio until he slid a Creedence Clearwater CD into the stereo and started swaying back and forth in the driver's seat, singing along to "Born on the Bayou." At one point a car pulled up alongside them, trying to pass on the right, and its driver, a teenager with a Mohawk, stared at Stony's father, laughing. He lowered his window and yelled something, which made Stony's father make a distorted face at the kid and say, "Duh . . ." Not surprisingly, the kid shot everyone the finger.

"Ah, the future of America," Stony's father said. He pushed a button to lower Sally's window and then yelled, "I'll see you the next time you pick up my garbage, son."

The kid peeled off, and Molly laughed.

"He's probably listening to that gangsta nonsense," Stony's father said. "You don't listen to that, do you, Stony?"

"Sometimes," Stony said.

"Stony likes the early alternative groups," Molly said, "like Nirvana and Pearl Jam."

"I didn't know that, Stony. I hope to discover all your secrets on this trip. I want us to be joined at the hip."

"You trying to make me jump out of the car?"

"I won't go back for you, you know."

"Sure you will. Who else would you torment?"

Sally sighed and Molly said, "This is going to be more fun than I thought."

"I'll need your help, Princess," their father said. "Stony's a formidable opponent."

"Too late, we already made a pact to gang up on you."

Sally leaned over and turned up the stereo just as "Who'll Stop the Rain" came on, and Stony found himself calming down, carried off to sleep by the monotonous rhythm of the car's motion and John Fogerty's voice.

Stony awoke as they glided into a rest stop close to the New York–Massachusetts border. It was almost noon.

"Chow time," his father said.

Molly groaned, stretching her legs out as far as she could, and Stony reached for a bottle of water he'd brought along.

"Sally wanted to make sandwiches," his father said, "but I told her, 'Nothing but the best for Stony and Molly.'"

"McDonald's?" Molly said.

Actually, Stony liked McDonald's, probably because his mother never let him eat there when he was a kid.

"Princess, you have to go no further than McDonald's to find America. Fake food for fat people on the run. And look," he said, pointing to a Starbucks sign. "Where else in the galaxy can you buy lunch for four bucks and thirty-five cents, then wash it down with a

Venti something or other for five thirty-five? You've got to love this country."

"You can always just get a salad," Sally said.

"Will you promise to inspect it for bugs? No, I want something that nukes all the germs out of it in a big vat of lard."

"You just want something to complain about," Sally teased.

"Untrue. It's not my fault I've been chosen to record the demise of America."

Stony laughed, and his father said, "Have your fun, Stony, but I'm the last man standing between McDonald's and the end of the world as we know it, though until then I'll take a Big Mac and a large order of fries." He opened his door, letting in a blast of hot, humid air.

Stony got out of the car and stretched. He could feel the heat rising off the blacktop, making everything appear filmy, somewhat surreal. He was hungry, and his father was right: a Big Mac sounded just perfect.

On their way into the rest stop, they had to pass a sunglasses vendor, and Molly and Sally tried on some of the odder designs.

"When women go on vacation, Stony," his father said, "they want to be adventurous, even if it's cheap sunglasses."

Sally overheard him and said, "Doesn't your head hurt from analyzing everything?" She tried on a pair with huge pink frames and white stars embedded in the plastic, then stuck her tongue out at him.

"Elton John is dead," his father said.

"That's a lie."

"Well, he should be."

"Let's get something to eat," Stony said, and he

and his father continued on toward the air-conditioned building.

On their way in, Stony saw a number of flyers that had been taped to the door, and on a table just inside the entrance was a big box of them. He and his father grabbed one. On the poster was a black-and-white photo of a teenage girl who appeared to be laughing. Her name was Britney Evans, and she was beautiful. She had lived around the area and had been missing for three months. His father read the details of her abduction, shaking his head. "She's probably dead by now," he said.

"Not necessarily."

"Are you clairvoyant?"

"Sometimes these girls run off with older men."

"How do you know that?"

"Because I've read about it."

His father looked discouraged. "This isn't about your weird books, Stony. It's about a dead girl."

"What weird books?"

"Look, I understand why you're reading them, but I don't think it's healthy, and your mother and I have spoken about it."

Stony was surprised, unaware that his mother had been poking around in his private library. Still, he felt the need to defend himself. "I want to be a lawyer," he said, "so I need to read about certain things."

"Like mass murderers?"

"That's an exaggeration."

"I'm not criticizing, Stony, just objecting to you making dumb comments about a missing girl."

Stony was somehow feeling guilty, but then that's how his father wanted him to feel. "Can we just get something to eat?"

"Sure," his father said. "But for the record, I think you'll be a great lawyer, and I hope you put scumbags who abduct young girls where they belong."

"Yeah, yeah," Stony said.

After they got their meals, Stony and his father sat down to eat. They didn't say much, but as Stony's father devoured his Big Mac, Stony noticed him glancing at a table about thirty feet away where two scruffy guys and a young Asian woman sat. His father began to talk about baseball, but it was clear he was fixated on the threesome.

"What's the matter?" Stony said. "You keep looking over there."

His father took a big sip from his root beer and folded his hands in front of him. "Just be quiet for a second and watch those three."

Stony repositioned his chair to see better.

On one side of the booth sat a big guy with a full red beard. His fleshy arms were completely exposed because of his blue tank top. He was pale, and it was clear he had recently been sunburned or boiled in oil. His curly red hair was shoulder-length and frizzy, and he had a blue handkerchief knotted around his skull. His face was so freckled it looked like he'd been stung by a thousand mosquitoes. He also seemed very strong, like one of those lumberjacks on TV, who could hurl barrels over their heads as if they were pieces of Styrofoam.

The other guy looked like he'd crawled out of an empty grave. He was skinny and dressed in black—black jeans, black engineer boots, and a black wifebeater. His hair was also black, long and stringy, tied back so tightly into a ponytail that it seemed to stretch the skin over his face, making him look embalmed. This tightness also accentuated his beak nose, and Stony wouldn't have been surprised if he had the ability to extend his tongue and capture bugs as they flew by.

Next to him was the Asian woman in a white smock dotted with small blue flowers. Unkempt and looking as if she hadn't washed her hair in days, she was hunched over, arguing with the thin man, but Stony couldn't understand her poor attempts at English. Every once in a while the thin man would elbow her in the ribs, making her wince, while the fat, red-headed man laughed a loud, throaty laughter as if trying to dislodge chunks of phlegm from his throat. Stony knew that if his father saw the thin man harassing the woman, there'd be trouble.

"How much you want to bet he bought her," his father said, taking a bite out of his hamburger and wiping some ketchup off his upper lip.

"What?"

"One of those mail-order jobs. These whack-a-doos get on the Internet and make contact with some poor woman who would rather get beaten over here than eat scraps of garbage the rest of her life."

"How could you possibly know that?"

"Look at her," he said. "They probably chain her up at night."

That thought made Stony feel a little sick inside. "It's none of our business," he said.

"I guess not." And his father looked away as Sally and Molly approached the table of strangers, carrying plastic dishes filled with salad. They were laughing, and when Molly playfully bumped into Sally, Sally dropped her salad onto the floor. The plastic container didn't break open but slid in the direction of the two men and the Asian woman. The man in black was up in an instant, slinking out of his booth and grabbing the container, then walking toward Sally. For the first time Stony got to see his whole face. He had such a narrow head that his dark eyes, sunk into deep grayish sockets, took up half his face. But he had a magnificent smile, as if every cent he ever made went into maintaining his teeth. He was taller and thinner than Stony had originally thought, and odd scribbling and symbols were tattooed on his arms. Stony also caught sight of his belt buckle, which bore the silver representation of a wolf.

Stony's father stood as the man neared Sally and handed her the salad. He spoke with her, then leaned over and whispered something into her ear, something that made her flinch. As she tried to walk away, he touched her hand, which brought Stony's father there in a second, followed by Stony. When the man saw them coming he moved away from Sally.

"It's okay, Art," Sally said.

"What's okay?" his father said, scrutinizing the man.

The man smiled.

"What's so funny, Queequeg?"

"Nothing," the man said. "I was just appreciatin' a beautiful woman."

"Well, go back to appreciatin' that poor thing over there," Stony's father said, gesturing toward the Asian woman. "And didn't your mother teach you not to touch strangers? You can get seriously hurt doing things like that."

The man wasn't smiling anymore, and the redheaded man inched himself out of the booth, joining his friend but not saying anything, just folding his arms and grinning. Stony knew something bad was going to happen, and the other patrons must have sensed trouble, too. They were filing out of the dining room, trying not to look behind.

Sally grabbed Stony's father's arm, saying, "Let's take our food outside."

"Please, Dad," Molly pleaded.

"I don't think King Arthur is going to do that," the man said, smiling again. "King Arthur wants to save a damsel in distress. " He bowed and grinned stupidly in Sally's direction, not out of respect but in a leering kind of way.

"Listen up, Queequeg," Stony's father said.

"The name's Leopold, and they call my friend Abraham."

"Listen up, Queequeg," Stony's father repeated. "I'll make this short. If you look at her like that again, I'm going to break one of your kneecaps, and when old Jethro comes at me I'll make sure he doesn't breathe right for two or three weeks."

"That would be impressive," the man said, seemingly unfazed by the threat. When Abraham laughed and moved closer, Stony picked up the faint odor of stale beer. Just as Abraham seemed ready to make his move, the man told him to go back to the table. "I think King Arthur means what he says," the man said. "So what happens now?"

"You're going to get your food and leave."

In spite of his size, the skinny man wasn't afraid. He kept nodding his head, staring right through Stony's father.

"Let's just move off, Dad," Stony said, "and give him a chance to leave."

"Smart boy," the man said, looking at Stony for the first time, who grabbed his father's arm and led him back to the table, followed by Sally and Molly.

When they sat down, Stony could see his father breathing heavily, fixating on the man in black, who moved slowly toward Abraham and the Asian woman. When the man reached the table, he said something to the woman, and then all three of them got up, taking what was left of their food. On the way out the thin man pushed the woman from behind, almost knocking her to the floor. He made a point of taunting Stony's father by smiling at him while lighting a cigarette. One of the counter people told him this was a no-smoking establishment, and he laughed, blowing smoke rings into the air.

"Was that really necessary?" Molly said. "Someone could've been hurt."

In contrast to Molly, Sally didn't criticize Stony's father. She seemed a bit shaken but also worried about him. "You okay?" she asked, touching his arm.

"What did he say?"

"He just picked up the salad, then asked where I was traveling to, and I told him Ashland, New Hampshire."

"Why did you tell him that?"

"He caught me off guard."

"What was he whispering to you?"

She blushed, then said, "Just sit," and he did.

After a few minutes, Stony's father calmed down, though Stony himself still felt shaky, wondering what Leopold and Abraham might do next. On their way out of McDonald's his father stopped in the small hallway between the restaurant and the glass doors leading outside. He was clearly wired, and in an attempt to relieve that pent-up energy, he grabbed a number of posters of the missing girl, then returned to the dining room and placed a poster on every empty table. Stony, Sally, and Molly watched, saying nothing.

Outside, the sun was so fierce, the air so humid, Stony could hardly breathe. When his father returned, all four of them stood near the sunglasses vendor, scanning the parking lot to see if Leopold had left, and it appeared he had. Stony felt his shoulders relax, but as they walked to the car, an old Ford Taurus station wagon veered their way. The car was dark brown and covered in places with lighter brown wood contact paper, as if the owner had really wanted to buy one of those old wood-paneled station wagons but couldn't afford it. On its hood was welded a huge ornament in the shape of a wolf. The strange silver figure would have been funny, but Stony noticed Leopold's sharp-beaked nose as the car passed. The Asian woman was sitting in the passenger side, and Abraham was jammed in the back with an assortment of clothes, blankets, and, strangely enough, a small gas grill, so that it seemed this threesome had everything they owned in the Taurus. The car glided by them, Leopold smiling, then shooting them the finger as he directed the Taurus onto the entrance ramp of the interstate.

And that's when it came to Stony, a vague recollection, a fleeting glimpse, of this man and the Taurus on the golf course when he had gone after reinforcements. How could they all have ended up in the same place again?

He waited for his father's reaction, fearing he'd chase down the station wagon and try to run it off the road. But, surprisingly, all his father said was, "There goes the Peacock family."

It took everyone a few seconds to get the joke, but eventually they laughed. When Stony and his sister were a few years younger they used to watch old *X-Files* DVDs with their parents, and there was one particularly scary episode about a genetically deficient Southern family who went around dismembering people. Everyone was so freaked out by the episode it became a family joke. His father even rented it for Sally so she wouldn't feel left out.

"If you ask me, they're creepier than the Peacock family," Sally said, "because they're real."

"I've seen those two guys before," Stony said.

"What?" his father said.

"At the golf course. They were parked behind the third green, watching you assault Al Capone. They were laughing at us."

Stony's father paused for a moment at the coincidence, then laughed. "Assault?"

"But I did see them."

"Well, you're probably mistaken," his father said, "but it's over, so everyone back in the car. We're not far from the Berkshires, and I've got a little game planned. Have you ever seen the Berkshires, Stony?"

"How would I have seen the Berkshires?"

"Don't you know not to answer a question with a question?"

And that's the way it went for the next fifty miles, with Stony's father laughing and telling everyone about the Berkshires, creating a question-and-answer kind of game where only he knew the answers.

"How high is the highest point of the Berkshires?" he'd ask, then imitate a buzzer and reveal the answer.

"Who did a classic study of vegetation in the Berkshires?"

"Audubon?" Molly suggested.

"*Bzzzz!* Good guess, Molly. It was a man named Egler."

"Who was Tanglewood named after?"

"What's Tanglewood?" Molly asked.

"It's where they hold a yearly music festival," Sally told her.

"*Bzzzz!* Nathaniel Hawthorne."

"That makes no sense," Stony said.

"It does if you know he wrote a collection called the *Tanglewood Tales*. Didn't you learn that at your expensive private school?"

"It's not like you're paying for it," Stony said, which was true. His and Molly's tuition came from money Stony's grandfather had left.

"Touché, d'Artagnan."

"Friend of the Three Musketeers," Stony said.

"Very good. How about this one? How many years ago were the Green Mountains and the Berkshires formed from prehistoric glaciers?"

"Three hundred fifty million years ago," Molly offered.

"Six hundred million," Sally said.

"Four hundred thirteen million, two months, and three days," Stony answered, making fun of the question.

"*Bzzzz!* Over a billion years ago," his father said, and the game, if you could call it that, went on for a good ten minutes, with Stony annoyed and surprised that his father had taken the time to memorize so much trivia.

The good thing about the game was that it provided a format where they could change topics from the Berkshires, which only his father knew about, to books or movies or actors and actresses. They would play for a while, take a break, and then someone would start a new category. They switched to books about ten miles before the exit to I-495.

"Who was the tattooed harpooner in *Moby-Dick*?" Stony asked.

"Queequeg," Molly answered.

"That's not fair," his father said. "You heard me call that creep Queequeg."

"Name one other harpooner," Stony said, "and you get to squeeze Dad's left ear until it bleeds."

"I wish I knew the answer to that question," Sally said, laughing.

"Whoa there," his father chimed in. "I'm actually a very nice guy."

After waiting a few seconds, Stony reluctantly sounded the buzzer. "Tashtego."

"You're kidding, right?" his father said.

"It's a very famous book."

"But it's a totally obscure question."

"More obscure than Tanglewood?"

Molly interrupted them, asking if she could have a bathroom break, so Stony's father pulled into a rest stop on the Mass Pike near a little town called Auburn. It was packed with cars, people wandering everywhere outside, sipping drinks on little patches of grass separating miniature pine trees. Stony was glad they stopped because his back was sore from being crammed in the rear seat. He also wanted something cold to drink, like a root beer.

They got out of the car, stretching and complaining about the heat, and that's when Stony saw it: the old Taurus. It was parked illegally on a little patch of road by the side of the restaurant, and the front passenger door was wide open, even though there was no one in the car. "Look," Stony said, gesturing toward it.

"Let's leave," Sally said.

"I can wait until the next rest stop," Molly added.

"We don't need to change our plans because of that mongoose," Stony's father said.

"Arthur," Sally warned.

"No trouble, I promise," he said, crossing his heart.

So everyone, except Stony's father, crept cautiously into McDonald's. Inside, Stony surveyed the crowd, but there was no sign of Leopold. He looked out the restaurant's window; the car was still there with its door open.

He bought a medium root beer while Sally and Molly went to the bathroom and his father wandered around trying to find the owners of the Taurus. Stony knew his father hadn't forgotten Leopold shooting him the finger, and he imagined him finding the culprit and bending back the offending digit until it broke. Then the cops would come, and Stony's father would be carted away while the whole "family trip" went down the drain. Stony was actually beginning to enjoy parts of it, and the thought of going home and hearing his mother carry on was unbearable.

He walked over to an arcade room next to the counter at McDonald's, stopping in front of a game with a rifle hanging from a rack. The goal was to see how many deer you could kill in two minutes. He grabbed the rifle and pointed it at a few stationary bucks, deciding whether to waste fifty cents.

"Two can play this game," a voice said from behind him. When Stony turned, he discovered his father grinning at him.

Stony looked at the rifle but couldn't muster up enthusiasm for shooting virtual deer.

"You're not one of those guys who think we should let deer run loose across America and starve to death, are you?"

Stony couldn't help but laugh, which made his father laugh, too.

"See, Stony, you're realizing I rarely take myself seriously."

"That's not true, though."

"You're probably right, but let's shoot these critters anyway until the ladies return."

But they never had a chance because Sally and Molly came out of the bathroom, and they weren't alone. The Asian woman who had been with Leopold accompanied them. She was shaking as Sally ushered her to a metal chair next to the Starbucks counter.

"They threw her out of the car," Sally said. "She was sitting on the floor of the bathroom crying. I asked her what happened, but she speaks little English."

"Then how do you know they threw her out of the car?" his father asked.

"She kind of mimicked it."

Stony looked closely at the woman. She was deathly thin, with faint bruises on her left leg and arm, as if she'd been elbowed or punched. The woman sounded like a wounded seal as she tried to explain something, but her laments made no sense. She frantically chattered on as travelers walked by. Two college-age guys started to laugh, and Stony told them to go to hell. His anger seemed to ignite his father, who went off to find Leopold. Stony followed him outside, but the car was gone, so they trotted off toward the gas pumps. It seemed as if Leopold and Abraham had left, already hurtling toward their next disaster.

"You go that way," his father said, pointing toward the interstate side of the parking lot, "and I'll backtrack the other way."

Stony did as he was told, walking very slowly, fearing that Leopold might leap out and smash him from behind with a hammer. Finally he met up with his father. "What should we do?"

"Let's go back inside."

When they returned, the Asian woman had calmed down, but Molly was crying, so Stony's father sat next to her and held her hand. "It's okay now."

"Okay? This is way too crazy."

"We can't leave her here," Sally said.

"Well, we can't take her on vacation with us," his father said. He let go of Molly and withdrew his cell phone from a holster attached to his belt, then called the police.

About five minutes later a state trooper arrived. Stony's father explained everything, but the trooper seemed skeptical. "Did anyone hit you?" he asked the woman, but she didn't answer.

"Of course someone hit her," Stony's father said. "Look at her arm and leg."

"Can someone calm this guy down," the trooper said, appealing to Sally. Then he asked the woman if she wanted to press charges. When he said that, it was clear she understood some English because she looked terrified. "No, no," she said, making a slicing motion with her hand under her neck.

"Look," Stony's father said, "while we're gabbing, those two creeps are getting farther away."

"I'm just trying to get information," the trooper said. "She won't or can't say what caused her injuries, and she's not interested in pursuing these guys."

"Just think out of the box for a second, will you."

This comment got under the trooper's skin, but he said he'd question her further at the station and decide what to do.

"Finally," his father said, and the trooper scowled at him.

"Where are her belongings?" the trooper asked.

"She didn't have any," Sally said.

"She doesn't have a purse?"

Sally shook her head.

"Great. Will you people step away for a moment and let me talk to her?" He sat next to the woman, trying to explain what was about to happen. After his explanation he thanked everyone, then asked to speak alone with Stony's father. He moved about twenty feet away, thinking no one could hear him. "I know you think you're trying to help," he said, looking very stern, "but in the future shut up once in a while." Then he returned and led the woman away. Before they reached the exit, the woman groaned, imploring Sally to go with her. Sally helplessly shrugged her shoulders.

"You've done more than enough," Stony's father said.

"I know, I know."

"What happens to someone like that?" Molly said. "It's just so sad."

"Whatever happens, she'll be taken better care of than when she was with those two hyenas."

Leopold watched their breasts rise and fall as they tried on sunglasses, laughing, while the blond man wrapped his arm around his woman's waist and the boy smiled, the kind of laughter he had grown up hating, the families at the county fair spreading out blankets and opening picnic baskets, as he looked on from behind a bush—at Darlene, for instance, with her red hair and pigtails, because she was the first, and who would have thought to look for a twelve-year-old boy

("It has to be a drifter," the police chief said), the town ignorant of snakes lying in wait beneath a rock or dropping from an overhead branch, no, he had no memories of laughter, even laughter like Abraham's, so full of menace, the trick being to enter the rest stop and slide by unnoticed, getting their food and drinks and then watch and wait, "Move it, or you'll be sleeping under the car with the mice tonight," giving the Asian woman a poke in the ribs, then sitting and shaping the legs and breasts of the woman and the girl on a paper napkin with a pencil stub he carried in his pocket, until the plastic container slid toward him, as if pushed by fate, coaxing him to follow the logic of the event, because the rest would be taken care of as long as he fixed his gaze on the chase and the flames, for he had decided on fire this time, and, finally, the showdown with the blond man, Leopold proud of his calmness, for calmness will lay great offenses to rest, *though he shouldn't have attracted attention, so he had to be punished, but how to pull off the road with the woman shrieking, "Now shut that woman up, Abraham," and he did, and then Leopold saying, "Right here, Abraham," pointing to his eye, Abraham striking him, then off until another stop, where they told her to clean up, not caring anymore to kill her properly, instead deserting her, only to stop in a little town a few miles away to catch their breath.*

No one had much to say when they resumed the trip. At first Molly wondered out loud about the Asian woman, but Sally changed the subject and passed around promotional pamphlets describing the condo where they would be staying and the surrounding attractions and restaurants. "There's kayaking just about everywhere," she said, "and there's supposed to be a cool little science center a few miles from the condo."

"And we can walk to the golf course, Stony," his father said.

Although Stony was most interested in golfing and kayaking, Molly was excited about a place called the Polar Caves. She grabbed a pamphlet from her purse and read a description of it.

"Sounds like fun," Stony said.

"Do I detect enthusiasm?" his father kidded.

"Maybe just a little."

"We'll be able to hike and explore there," Molly added.

Stony tried to pay attention as everyone went through their itineraries for the vacation, but he couldn't shake the image of the Asian woman as the trooper led her away. He felt that in a few years, with no place to go and not knowing anyone, she'd be found dead in an alley in some city. He imagined Leopold and Abraham, like those twisted people he had read about, already off the interstate, raping and pillaging, or at least dismembering a few cats. Disturbed by these possibilities, he mentally escaped to one of his favorite countries, which he had Googled at home: Greece.

He pictured himself sitting beneath a relief sculpture of Dionysus at the Parthenon. He is tired from the climb to the monument, and the sun is very hot. He opens a lunch he has prepared for himself—a salad with olives and feta cheese, washed down with some retsina—while tourists mill about, speaking an assortment of foreign languages. He is far away from home, happy to be on his own. No parents, no bad memories. The sun is blinding, but from the corner of his eye he sees her, tall and olive-skinned, with long black hair cascading down the back of her loose-fitting white blouse, through which he can see the outlines of her bra. Her name is Ianthe, and she is wearing a long rose-colored peasant skirt that ends a foot above her sandals, whose top straps are embedded with matching green stones. When the breeze passes over her, her skirt clings to her inner thighs and she keeps it from climbing up her legs by holding her palms tightly to her quads. She is standing by herself, staring out toward the Mediterranean, and Stony says the one word he knows, *Kalimera*, which means hello.

When she turns toward him, he half expects a trio of musicians to appear, strumming odd-looking stringed instruments and singing folk songs, but the sound of her voice is enough. And of course she laughs at his attempt to speak Greek, because, in fact, she is fluent in English, having attended boarding schools in London. Later, they plan to meet at the base of Mount Lykavettos, where she leads him through shrubs and small trees toward stone stairs that zigzag upward, as she tells him the story of how the goddess Athena dropped this mountain accidentally before reaching the Acropolis. And he will believe most anything she says as they sit at a café, surveying the neighborhoods below and the ships leaving for the islands. That night she will meet him, not at one of the clubs, but in a secluded place by the sea . . .

Stony knew where this reverie would lead, and he was more than happy to go there until he heard his father suddenly yell, "What the hell?" followed by Molly saying, "Oh, no. Oh, no," and then Sally screaming at his father to speed up.

When Stony came out of his daydream he saw his father adjusting the rearview mirror and Molly and Sally gaping in astonishment behind them. Stony turned to see what the drama was: a dead deer? (but he had felt no crash); an errant mattress improperly tied down on the hood of a car? (but his father had not swerved). And that's when he saw the Taurus, the color of dog scat, no more than five feet behind them. The car was so close he could see a fresh cut over Leopold's eye, so close he could make out the grotesque features of the hood ornament. His father had to be going at least 75, but the old Taurus kept pace behind them. Leopold was laughing and sticking out his tongue, apparently bent on slamming into the Highlander and killing everyone.

"Hold on to something," Stony's father said. "I'm going hit the brakes and make that bastard crash."

"I don't think he'll care," Stony said.

"Stony's right," Sally said, reaching for her cell phone. As she did, Leopold suddenly decelerated, the Taurus looking as if some force was slowly pulling it out of sight.

"Put down the phone," Stony's father said. "What are you going to tell the cops, that someone's tailgating us?"

"We have to do something," Sally said.

"I think they had their fun."

But Stony's father was wrong. Just as suddenly as the Taurus had disappeared, it was accelerating toward them. Stony felt certain that this time Leopold planned to ram them, the quickness of his approach suggesting that he had to be going at least 90.

"Just everyone brace themselves," his father said, and they all faced forward, awaiting the crash, trying to grip something. But instead of the sound of the Taurus's grille totaling the back of the Highlander, they heard a prolonged high-pitched, angry wail. When Stony found the courage to turn around, the Taurus was again about five feet behind them, with Leopold laying on his horn.

Just as he had customized the Taurus with cheap contact paper and the wolf hood ornament, he had installed a siren. Stony stared at Leopold, whose face was frozen in rage, and he wondered what would happen next. Much to his surprise, the Taurus swerved dangerously to the right. Stony was sure it would overturn, but Leopold maneuvered it safely onto an exit ramp.

"It's over," Stony said. "They got off the interstate."

Molly's hands were shaking, and Sally frantically punched the keys of her cell phone. Meanwhile, his father pulled onto the shoulder, banging his fist hard against the dashboard. "That crazy bastard," he said, taking a few calming breaths. Then he gently removed the cell phone from Sally's hand. "Nothing will come of that."

"He could have killed us," Sally said.

"She's right, Dad," Stony said.

"It's our word against his, and he's gone now. We'll be out of reach in another half hour."

"But he knows where we're going," Sally said.

"She's right," Stony added.

"Stony," his father said, "with Sally scared and your sister in tears, I hope you aren't going to argue with me." He appeared exasperated, looking from Sally to Molly, then back at Stony. He stared into the rearview mirror for a moment. "Look, if we see that car again, I promise to call the troopers, but, really, what can they do. No one's been hurt, and any witnesses are already five miles down the interstate."

Stony knew his father was right, but there was something about Leopold that defied normal logic.

"Look," his father said, "we don't have far to go, so let's salvage the day." Then he steered the car back onto the interstate, accelerating. An uncomfortable silence filled the car for a few minutes until Stony's father said, "Was it actors or actresses?" referring to the game they had been playing. Everyone seemed relieved and ready to join in, though Stony couldn't help periodically glancing behind. From the reading he'd done, he believed that once people like Leopold decided to hate someone, they didn't stop until they hurt them in some very ugly way. But at least they were safe for now, though Stony could see a change in his father. In the past, Stony had seen his father verbally spar with a number of tough guys, but Leopold had thrown him a curve, and even as he tried to stump them with difficult questions, he frequently adjusted the rearview mirror, and his voice lacked its usual cockiness.

Shortly after crossing the New Hampshire border, they pulled into a rest stop situated on top of a hill. Unlike the others, this one had no McDonald's or Starbucks or Nathan's Famous Hot Dogs, just a state liquor store, restrooms, and a lot of vending machines.

"This is my kind of state," his father said. "The lousy food is where it belongs—locked up in machines."

"But I *am* hungry," Molly said.

"I have a lot of change," Sally offered. "Why don't we get some snacks while your dad and Stony buy a nice bottle of Chablis."

"Can we have a glass?" Molly asked.

Sally looked at Stony's father. "I don't think a small glass with dinner will hurt."

"Kids drink wine in Europe all the time," Molly offered.

His father laughed. "As long as they don't tell their mother, I don't care."

"We won't, will we, Stony?"

"Mom wouldn't mind," Stony said, defensively. "You don't have to make her sound like a prude."

"If there's any question about it," Sally said, "I'll call her."

"Okay, okay," his father said.

They all got out of the car and stretched. While they were driving, a weak cold front had passed through, bringing a refreshing breeze. According to Stony's calculations, they'd been on the road for nine hours and had only about an hour left. In the distance Stony could see clusters of pine trees shrinking beneath a setting sun. Before he and his father walked to the liquor store, his father opened the hatch of the Highlander and rummaged through the back, digging out some binoculars.

"What are those for?" Stony asked.

"See that little rise over there?" his father said, pointing toward a hill to the left of the liquor store. "After we get the wine, let's plop down and look at the view."

"While you're doing that, we'll eat our snacks over there," Sally said, gesturing toward picnic tables next to the tourist information booth.

"Sounds like a plan," his father said.

After buying the wine, Stony and his father climbed the rise and sat down on a huge boulder half buried in the ground. His father lifted the binoculars to his eyes, but he wasn't facing the beautiful winding river snaking its way through a little valley or the scenic foothills off to the north. Instead, the binoculars were aimed toward the interstate.

"You're looking for them, aren't you?"

"Yeah, but don't say anything to Sally or Molly."

"So you're worried?"

"There's something wrong with that skinny guy. He's not wired right. I don't know how to put it."

"Are you scared?"

His father still had the binoculars to his eyes. "You always worry about your family."

Stony laughed.

"I know what you think, Stony—about a lot of things—but someone would have to kill me before I'd let them hurt you."

He lowered the binoculars and stared hard at Stony, who couldn't remember the last time he had locked eyes with his father. They normally existed in each other's peripheral vision, which partly accounted for the discomfort Stony felt around his father.

"I know I haven't always been there," his father said, "especially after your grandmother was murdered."

"You've never even talked to me about it," Stony said.

"It's not my way."

"But you could've tried to explain."

"Explain what? That some crazy guy stabbed your grandmother because God or Satan told him to, or because he was reliving some battle from Vietnam? How can you explain something so cruel and pointless?"

His father placed his hand on Stony's knee. He squeezed it lightly, surprising Stony. "Let's face it. I'm never going to be the dad you want. Yeah, I've screwed up, but don't expect me to torture myself the rest of my life."

"Even a few weeks would be nice."

"You're pretty unforgiving for a young guy. I was hoping we might get closer on this trip."

"In one lousy week?"

His father raised the binoculars to his eyes again,

back to his old self. "You'll have to bag that anger someday."

"Geez," was all Stony could come up with.

For about ten silent minutes, Stony and his father took note of the passing traffic, then climbed down the rise and joined Sally and Molly.

"I saved some chips for you," Molly said, "and we bought some Cokes."

While Stony opened his drink and ate some chips, he noticed his father staring oddly at him. "What?" Stony said.

"Just looking at you. You're a handsome guy, you know?"

"Don't tell me you two were bonding up there," Molly teased.

His father didn't answer. He patted Stony on the shoulder and told everyone to get back into the car. "Just a little longer," he said, "and then Shangri-La."

The sky was a cloudless dark blue. It was about six p.m. After everyone got settled in the condo, Stony and his father decided to rent a video, so they tramped up a paved road leading to the condominium office. While his father went inside, Stony walked around the grounds for about fifteen minutes, finally peering over a tall fence at a good-sized pool, shaped in a figure eight. Off to the side of the diving board was a smaller swimming area for children, and behind that a circular whirlpool, which could fit about four people. In it, a bald, hairy guy was floating on his back, though none of the jets were working. His legs bobbed up and down as he waved his arms from side to side. In the back corner of the pool area was a long, rectangular concrete shuffleboard where two boys of about ten launched pucks at each other, more intent on causing bodily harm than scoring points. A few mothers in one-piece bathing suits sprawled in adjustable white lounge chairs encircling the pool.

Having seen enough, he entered the office. His father was at the video collection, talking to a girl about Stony's age, whose beauty froze him. Her hair, burnt auburn, was wet and stringy from the pool, and she had a dark blue towel wrapped around her waist, so all Stony could see was the top of her two-piece bathing suit, which was navy blue, exposing a few inches of cleavage. He found himself lingering on a reddish birthmark the size of a quarter floating above her left breast. When he looked up, she was smiling at his fixation, and he felt his face go red.

"I was just talking about you," his father said.

"What a surprise," Stony said, making the girl laugh. She had perfectly formed teeth, and when she smiled it was as if two Ping-Pong balls inflated inside her cheekbones. But it was her eyes, the color of pine, that dazzled him.

"Your father said you're an angry guy."

Stony could only sigh.

"What I said is my son is smart, handsome, and athletic, but he has a problem with anger and reads weird books."

"How did he get to my legendary anger and reading habits in just fifteen minutes?" Stony asked.

"You know how I babble," his father said, "especially around cute girls."

The girl seemed surprised by this confession and scratched her head. "Maybe we should start with something normal, like your name."

"Stony," he said.

"Where did you get a name like that?"

"His grandfather," Stony's father said.

Stony laughed. "Have you noticed that when I talk, my words come out of my father's mouth?"

The girl laughed too, a big, beautiful laugh. Stony was more than willing to be funny for the next hundred years if he could keep her laughing.

"Really, though," she said, "where did you get it?"

"My father's right. My grandfather's name was Elston, so I was named after him, but it got shortened to Stony because my father thought everyone would make fun of Elston."

"Which was true," his father said.

"Well, whatever the reason," the girl said, "I like it." She loosened her towel, trying to rearrange it, exposing two very strong legs and a tiny waist. "Do you guys go on like this all the time?"

"Actually, we hardly see each other."

"That's not true," his father said, winking at the girl. Then he grabbed Stony around the waist and gave him a bear hug.

"Don't you have something to do?" Stony said.

Stony's father looked at him, then the girl. "I get it," he said. "But make sure to grab a good movie." Before he left, he said, "Aren't you going to tell us your name?"

Stony cringed at the "us."

"It's Ruth."

"That's pretty," his father said, before slapping Stony on the back and leaving.

With his father's departure there seemed to be more oxygen in the room, and he and the girl gave a collective sigh.

"He's an odd guy," Ruth said. "Is he always that hyper?"

"Most of the time," Stony said, annoyed that they were talking about his father. "Everyone's parents are a little weird, though, don't you think?"

Her smile became a frown. "I wouldn't know. I don't have a father, and don't want to talk about it."

"I didn't ask you to."

"You would have. Whenever a guy finds out my father split he wants to know why. Then he wants to be my big brother or come on to me."

"Geez," Stony said. "Maybe I should go for something normal too, like how you got *your* name."

"My mother, believe it or not, is very religious. Ruth means 'friend,' so I'm supposed to have a lot of sympathy and pity for people. In short, if you want sympathy or pity, I'm your girl."

"Well, you met my father, so you know I need sympathy."

"Ha," Ruth said, then pointed to rows of DVDs in the bookshelves behind her. "Why don't we find you a movie. I'm getting a little cold here, and I'd like to change out of this suit." She snapped one of her straps, a gesture that seemed perfectly natural. She bent over to look at the DVDs, and when Stony crouched next to her he could smell the pool's chlorine. He was hoping it would take long to find a good movie, afraid she'd hand him a DVD and vanish in a puff of smoke.

The bookshelves were separated into three categories: Adult, Family, and "Kiddies."

"You probably want a family movie, right?"

Stony would've rather watched a thriller or action movie, but most of them had sex scenes, and he wouldn't have felt comfortable seeing those with Sally. "Yeah, that's probably best."

"They have some good ones," she said. She knelt

on the floor, pulling out DVDs and replacing them. Stony knelt with her.

"You must vacation here a lot."

"One week a year. They don't change a lot of these movies, so I've probably seen most of them." She removed one, seeming content with the choice. It was *Nim's Island.*

"Isn't that kind of corny?"

She looked surprised. "If you think a girl trying to save her father and protect animals is corny."

"Sorry," he said.

She laughed and poked him in the shoulder. "It's actually a funny movie, but I bet you'll all be crying at the end."

Stony had trouble imagining himself and his father huddled on the floor, weeping.

Ruth handed him the DVD. "What are you doing tonight?" she asked.

As an answer, Stony held up the movie.

"How about tomorrow?"

"We're supposed to go to the Polar Caves."

"Could we meet afterwards, downstairs, about six? There's a Ping-Pong table and some video games. Now I really have to get out of these clothes," she said, suddenly unwrapping the towel and draping it around her shoulders, then turning and disappearing quickly down a hallway where Stony assumed the showers were.

After Ruth left, he brought the DVD to the counter. A woman about sixty was sitting at a desk, playing solitaire on a computer. She had silver hair pulled back into a ponytail, and she wore small, dark pink plastic bifocals. She was the same receptionist Stony and his father had met when they signed in.

"Did you find a good one?" she said pleasantly.

"I had some help."

"Yeah, that one's a real trip."

"What do you mean?"

The woman seemed sorry she'd spoken. "No, not like that. I've just seen guys act dopey around her since she was twelve."

Stony wanted to ask the woman if Ruth ever hooked up with any of these guys. He wanted to know if that's what she was hinting at, but he didn't know how to ask a question like that. The woman must have noted his disappointment because she said, "Don't mind me, sweetie. I shouldn't be talking about vacationers, anyway."

"She seems nice to me," Stony said.

The woman took the video from him and began to write something in a little book. "The thing I like about her is she can take care of herself. She's pleasant, even a bit flirtatious, with the younger guys, but they always leave the office empty-handed, or maybe I should say empty-headed." She laughed loudly at her joke. "You want to charge this to your condo?"

Stony didn't answer. He was thinking of Ruth.

The woman handed the video back to him and said, "I was surprised because I've never heard her make a date."

Stony wondered if he should be mad at the woman's eavesdropping, but then, what else can you do sitting at a counter all day?

"Well, try to have fun," she said, winking at him. "You two look cute together."

Stony felt himself blush.

"A grown boy blushing," she said. "Now that's refreshing."

"Ha," Stony said, before saying goodbye.

Everyone was tired and hungry in the morning but eager to visit the Polar Caves. After showering, they left, taking the interstate to a smaller route spotted with convenience stores and a few doughnut shops.

Stony's father sighed. "Here we are in God's country and can't find an old-fashioned pancake house with steak and eggs and flapjacks soaked in maple syrup." He was wearing tan hiking shorts, a blue T-shirt, and a pair of gray New Balance running shoes. On his head was a Buffalo Bisons hat turned backwards.

"I'm sure there are tons of great places," Sally said.

"But it looks like Dunkin' Donuts for now," his father said, pulling into a parking lot with a fresh layer of blacktop.

The day was unusually dry, though a few large clouds floated above. Everything around them—the mountains, the trees, even the little stores—had a sharp outline. Stony hadn't slept too well, his dreams shot through with images of Leopold and Abraham but also of Ruth, so this weather was welcome. Stony trailed behind as his father, Sally, and Molly walked toward Dunkin' Donuts. He thought outsiders would probably call them a "handsome family." Even with little or no makeup, Sally and Molly were beautiful and could've easily passed for mother and daughter. Molly wore a snug light green T-shirt and new blue mid-thigh shorts. On her feet were dark purplish hiking boots.

Sally's boots looked much traveled, as did her tan cargo shorts. She too wore a green T-shirt, one that she had purchased at an Army-Navy store. Her hair was drawn into a ponytail, which she had threaded through the adjustable band of a tan baseball cap. It was clear who would be leading the hikes on this trip.

"I'm glad you bought those boots," Stony said to Molly. "If we get lost at night we won't need a flashlight."

"Well, aren't you the comedian," his father said. "It's amazing how one little girl can change a guy's life."

"What girl?" Molly asked.

"I'll tell you about it while we're eating our greasy doughnuts."

Sally halted, waiting for Stony to reach her. "Don't worry, I'll protect you."

"I hope you brought your Uzi."

The menu at Dunkin' Donuts wasn't what they had hoped for, but the coffee was good. As they stood at the counter and drank, they took their time scanning the food choices on the wall.

"What's in a Spanish cheese croissant?" Stony's father asked a long-haired kid behind the counter.

"I'll have to ask the manager, sir," he said, and walked toward a guy working the drive-through window.

"Don't they train kids anymore?" Stony's father said.

"I have this great idea," Stony said. "Why don't you be nice to the kid instead of embarrassing Molly and me."

His father looked puzzled, then surprised Stony by saying, "All right, I get it."

The kid returned and said, "The manager had to leave, but from my experience, it's tasty."

Stony cringed, waiting for his father's next salvo, but instead he smiled broadly and said, "That's good enough for me, son." Then he looked at Stony. "How was that?"

"Just the right blend of enthusiasm," Stony said.

The kid looked confused but then fell into his role as everyone ordered something. While they were waiting for their muffins to heat up, Stony heard a person farther along the counter, an older guy, telling their server about a kid who'd been shot the previous night while hitchhiking to his home, which was about ten miles north. Stony's father heard the conversation, too, and said, "You have to be nuts to hitchhike nowadays."

The guy who related the story shuffled toward them. He was skinny with thinning black hair, which he combed over his bald spot, and above his lip was a black Hitler-style mustache. "Around here, kids hitchhike all the time," he said.

"It's still nuts to me."

The guy nodded. "The weird thing is that the kid had traveled all the way from Memphis by bus, then gets shot ten miles from home. The cops said he hadn't been robbed. Just one bullet in the chest. Makes no sense."

"You wouldn't think that could happen up here," Sally said.

"I guess it can happen anywhere," the guy said.

"Do they have any suspects?" Stony asked.

"They didn't say much, but it must be personal. It was probably someone whose girlfriend he was banging." He looked at Molly and Sally and turned red. "Sorry, ladies, that just came out."

"That's okay," Sally said.

While they were talking, the kid with the long hair handed their orders to Stony's father, and the older guy said, "Enjoy your breakfast."

They drifted toward a table and sat down, still talking about the shooting. "Let's ask the Professor of Evil," his father said.

"I don't know about Stony," Sally said, "but I'm pretty sick of this badgering, Arthur." Sally normally didn't come on so strong, but when she did, Stony's father always clammed up.

"No, I don't mind," Stony said. "If you want to really understand my 'fascination with evil,'" Stony added, making imaginary quotation marks in the air, "I'll tell you the difference between this shooting and what I've read about. There's probably a reason this kid was killed, based on what he did to someone or because of some grudge. I mean, it can be explained. What freaks me out is the kind of violence that has no logic."

"That's all you learned from your books?" his father asked.

"No, but it's too complicated to go into."

"Sounds like a term paper to me," his father said.

"Arthur," Sally warned.

"It's okay," Stony said. "It *was* from a term paper. A pretty good one, too."

Molly took a bite out of her muffin, looking bored by the conversation. "Let's change the subject," she said. "I want to know about Stony's girlfriend."

Stony groaned. "She's just a girl I met when I got the video."

"What's her name?" Sally asked.

"Ruth."

"That's pretty."

"Are you going to see her again?"

"Maybe tonight, but it's no big deal."

Stony's father laughed.

"What?" Stony asked.

"Look, it's none of my business, but there were big-time sparks flying yesterday."

"Is she pretty?" Molly asked.

"Let's just drop it," Stony said.

"But I want to know more."

"Look," Stony added, "I promise to give you all a report after tonight."

"But you won't," Molly complained.

"And that will be just fine," Sally said.

"Well, let's finish up here," Stony's father said. "The Caves open at nine a.m., so if we get there fast, we won't have to deal with a bunch of tourists."

There was always an untraveled dirt road to pull into, where you could block the opening with thick branches, moss-covered logs, and spend the night curled up in the front seat, hoping something might happen, just to keep the edge up, one time opening a can of beans and placing it on the hood, thinking a bear might show, "And then what? And then what, Abraham?," Abraham laughing, both of them knowing it was always best to have cans of tuna and beans, best sometimes not to start a campfire, especially now, so as to keep low until the killing was done, and so they were looking for a lair on an unlit country road when they almost ran down a humpbacked figure, then turning around to make another pass, driving slowly toward the shape, Abraham laughing, "Lookee here, a hitchhiker," Leopold knowing the old game, and when they reached him, "No, not a man but a boy" (Leopold thinking of the other boy), Abraham rolled down his window, laughing, as Leopold peeled away, because why hurt this boy and bring in the police, but then the boy made that gesture and swore (like the blond man insulting his mama), Leopold hearing those words and these, Do not take revenge but leave room for God's wrath, *but what God?, so he doubled back, driving slowly toward the figure, Abraham removing the gun from the glove compartment, the sound of its report echoing in Leopold's ears, so used to it he never flinched.*

Later, stretched out in the front seat, the night alive with the chatter of crickets, one bright star throbbing through an opening in the trees, he has a dream where he's falling through a night sky, staring at that star, waiting for a huge black bird to snatch him in its claws.

"You stand in the middle," Stony's father said. "Drape your arms around Sally's and Molly's shoulders. Don't worry, you won't melt. Now, everyone say 'cheese.'"

Stony's father snapped a few pictures, then switched places with Stony. Finally, Molly made Stony pose with his father, asking them to lock arms. "Just two old buddies," she joked. Later, Stony looked at the picture, his father smiling broadly, him pursing his lips as if he'd just sucked on a pickle.

They were all posing under a sign saying THE POLAR CAVES, the words carved separately on three rough planks attached to a log with thin chains. Both ends of the log were embedded in pyramid-shaped man-made rock structures. Off to the side was another, smaller sign: *The Polar Caves were formed about fifty thousand years ago as the third continental glacier descended over New Hampshire's White Mountains. When the ice retreated, it left behind an amazing series of caves and passageways for visitors to explore. Self-guided tours take you to the rock garden and nature trails and through the caves.*

Stony's father was right about arriving early. There was only one other car in the parking lot, a van that unloaded a couple and their two young children. The whole family was overweight, and Stony wondered how they would fit through the caves. He had read that some were very narrow. There was even one called the "The Lemon Squeeze."

His father noticed the family. "Let's move it," he said, grabbing a backpack that had been on the floor in front of Sally. "Probably not a good idea to get behind that crew."

They hurried up a wood-chip path to a lodge that sold all kinds of rocks and crystals.

"Geez," his father said, looking around, "chachkas everywhere. What a country."

"They're more than just chachkas," Molly said, and she was right. The floor was made of smooth granite slabs expertly melded together and grouted. Neatly spaced on the floor were long glass display cases containing polished gems, dragons crafted from pewter, Russian dolls, and a variety of ceramic trolls, all of which glimmered under the bright lights.

Molly was toying with a chess set made from various crystals when Stony's father pressured everyone to follow him to the ticket counter, manned by a kid about Stony's age. He wore a blue T-shirt with Polar Caves etched in white over his left breast. Longish blond hair spilled out of his blue baseball cap, which had a tiny polar bear stitched on front. He was a big kid, very athletic, with a tuft of hair sprouting from under his lip and biceps that stretched the arms of his T-shirt. He was fixated on Molly, and Stony's father seemed to notice, looking a bit amused. He took out his wallet. "Fifteen bucks apiece? For that I better get to wrestle a polar bear."

The kid smiled, glancing at Molly again, who blushed. When they left the lodge, Stony's father laughed loudly.

"Don't say it," Molly said.

"Say what?"

"Say what you're going to say."

"But don't you think it's funny we're here for less

than twenty-four hours and everyone's falling in love with my children?"

"It's far from love," Molly protested.

"Well, it's hard for a father to see a godlike young man lusting after his daughter."

"The dude did light up in your presence," Stony added.

"And I don't blame him," Sally said. "She's a beautiful girl. Now leave her alone and let's get moving or your father will end up complaining about something else."

The path from the lodge led to a covered bridge. As they crossed it, Stony heard Sally ask his father if he was sure he was "okay with this."

"Shhh," his father said. "This is all Molly's been talking about." He turned to see if Stony had overheard, and Stony pretended he hadn't, though he couldn't imagine what Sally meant.

After the bridge there was a long flight of wooden stairs leading up to the caves. It was a steep climb but pleasant. The surrounding trees broke any wind, so conditions were perfect—cool, yet comfortable enough for shorts and a T-shirt. Sunlight filtered through the trees, giving a primeval feel to the landscape. Higher up, where the temperatures were even cooler, the light shone through mist as if through stained-glass windows, creating a rainbow effect.

They came to a rock garden of big boulders, transformed into odd shapes by prehistoric glaciers. They were named after profiles of famous people or animals they resembled. In between these moss-covered monstrosities, boardwalks had been constructed so seamlessly they looked like they'd been there since the retreat of the glaciers.

When they left the rock garden and climbed toward the first cave, Sally pressed his father again, but he waved her off. At the entrance he said he'd go first, and Sally looked concerned. "If there are any bear in here, buckeroos, I'll let you know," Stony's father joked.

"That's not possible, is it?" Molly asked.

"Of course not," Sally said, but Stony wondered if there might be other varmints or rodents, though growing up in the city, he wouldn't have known the difference between a mole and a possum.

His father entered the cave with Molly and Sally behind him. Before Stony could climb down the stairs, his father had already popped out the other end about thirty feet away. He stumbled a few times, gasping for air.

"You okay?" Stony asked.

He nodded, sitting down on the platform. "Fine. Just a little dizzy. Go in, it's fun."

"You sure?"

Just then Sally emerged from the cave. She seemed irritated. "Just go, Stony, so your sister's not alone."

At first his eyes had trouble adjusting to the darkness. Light from the outside trickled in as he descended, the air becoming damper until he reached a flat area illuminated by an electric bulb hooked up in the cave's darkest corner. It was a tight fit, but he was able to move around fairly comfortably. This cave was even large enough to house a little bench, so you could sit and wait for a spider to come along and weave its web. After a minute or two he followed Molly out of the cave into the sunlight, where they found their father sipping from a water bottle.

They drifted from cave to cave, Stony's father always insisting on going first, exiting way ahead of everyone. Each cave was a bit tighter than the last, and after each exit his father appeared drained, which surprised Stony because he was in such good shape. Periodically, one cave would have an alternate passageway that was easier. There was one called the Party Pooper and another the Chicken Walk, but Stony's father urged them to take the harder route, even though Sally didn't want to. "It's important Molly has the whole experience," he said.

"Well, you don't have to be a part of it," Sally replied.

"Is your back sore or something?" Molly asked.

"I'm fine," Stony's father said, and Sally shook her head.

Finally they came to a cave with two routes, the Orange Crush and the Lemon Squeeze. His father took a deep breath, and Sally said to Stony, "I think you and your sister should do the Lemon Squeeze, and your father and I will tackle the other one."

"No way," Stony's father said, dropping down into the cave before anyone could stop him.

Within a few minutes they were all inside. The first section was easy, illuminated by rays of natural sunlight and large enough to fit them all, but travel ahead became tighter and darker with no visible exit. Stony could sense that his father was uncomfortable. He was jabbering, making little jokes that made no sense, and he kept zipping and unzipping little pockets of the backpack he had removed.

"You okay, Dad?" Molly asked.

When his father didn't respond, Sally took the backpack from him and headed toward the vein that led out. "Let me go first," she said, and Stony's father followed her, shadowed by Stony, with Molly bringing up the rear. Struggling through the passageways, his T-shirt damp from the moisture on the walls, Stony could see why they called it the Lemon Squeeze. To make matters worse, his father seemed to be lurching forward only an inch at a time, gasping for air. Finally, they came to a halt, and Stony heard Sally's frantic voice. "Arthur?"

There was no answer, and although his father's running shoes were twitching, he wasn't advancing.

"Molly, Stony, back up fast," Sally said.

"What's wrong?" Molly said.

"Just do it," Stony said. He saw Molly's silhouetted shape disappear behind him, and he moved crablike toward a shaft of light at the cave's opening, where he waited with Molly until his father wriggled out of the narrow crevice, looking terrified as he crawled hastily on all fours toward the exit, followed by Sally. By the time Molly and Stony climbed onto the boardwalk, he was leaning on a wooden railing, gulping water, obviously shaken. His right knee was bleeding, and Sally, on her knees, was cleaning the wound, reaching into a first-aid kit she had brought. His father seemed embarrassed but was making the best of it.

"You're not having a heart attack, are you?" Molly asked. She looked like she was going to cry.

Stony's father laughed, which seemed to settle him. "I wish," he said.

"You're claustrophobic, aren't you," Stony said.

"Bravo, Stony."

"Claustrophobic?" Molly said.

"Yes, Princess. My Achilles' heel."

"For how long?" Stony asked.

"For as long as I've been alive." He continued to drink from his water bottle. "Think back. Whenever I took you guys to a movie, where did we sit?"

"Aisle seats in the back," Molly said.

"Same thing at a sporting event. And why do you think I insist on driving all the time?"

It was beginning to come together in Stony's mind—all the events his father wouldn't attend, like parent lunches, and why he probably became a house painter, so he could move around as he pleased. Stony imagined his father arriving early for law school, hoping to find a seat by an exit in the crowded lecture hall.

His father screwed the top onto his bottle and smiled. "Now you're one up on me, Stony."

"I'm not like that," Stony said.

"But it must be nice to know I have my weaknesses."

Stony almost laughed, and Sally said what he was thinking. "I'm sure he's already aware of them, Arthur."

"Then why did you come here?" Molly asked. "I told you what the caves were like."

"Because you wanted to."

Molly went over and hugged him.

"Enough," he said emphatically, kissing her on the forehead. "Now we know your dad's a control freak and a wussy boy." He looked over at the opening of the Lemon Squeeze. "But I need to go back in there."

"Forget it," Molly protested. "We've done enough."

"But we almost finished it."

"This is stupid," Sally said.

"I'll go with you," Stony said, surprising himself.

Before Sally could argue, Stony's father had climbed back down, Stony behind him. They never said a word to each other, just clawed and crawled their way through the clammy narrow crevices with the speed and dexterity of trolls. When they exited, Molly and Sally were waiting anxiously for them. "You're nuts," Molly said.

His father looked a bit weary but pleased with himself. "Thanks, Stony."

"No problem," Stony said.

After finishing their trek through the caves, they hiked a short, easy trail circling the park. Realizing they hadn't eaten since breakfast, they left around 11:30, almost stopping at a Burger King, but Sally argued that it was time for "real food," so Stony and his father said they'd find a market. They also needed to buy golf balls somewhere.

Stony and his father dropped off Sally and Molly back at the condo and then checked in at the office, getting directions to a little mall that featured a supermarket and an Olympia Sports, over near the interstate. The directions took them onto a country road dotted with an odd mixture of houses—classic colonials situated only three hundred yards from trailer homes ringed with rotting carcasses of cars or pickup trucks.

"I'll bet the gene pool's a little thin in that establishment," Stony's father said, pointing to one of the trailer homes.

Stony laughed. "Did I ever tell you about Grandpa and me golfing in Eden, New York?"

"Which grandpa?"

"*Your* dad," Stony said.

"Let's hear it."

"It was about five years ago, right before he got sick. You know that course, the one surrounded by cow pastures?"

"Yeah, he really liked that place."

"On the way there his car broke down, so we were stuck on Route 5 until AAA came. He got freaked out by being in the boondocks, and you know what he asked me?"

"What?"

"He said, 'You think it's safe here or should we call your father?' And I said, 'Why wouldn't it be safe?' And he said, 'Well, you know, *Deliverance*.' It took me a while to figure out what he was talking about, but then I realized he thought hillbillies might leap out of the bushes and, well, you know."

"Do the nasty with him?"

"Yeah."

Stony's father smiled. "Did you ever ask him if he looked in the mirror?"

They both laughed as they turned onto another route, passing a big barn where used cars were sold. There was a huge sign out front that read, *We finance everyone. No questions asked.* They were almost past the place when Stony yelled, "Stop."

"What?"

"Just pull over."

His father directed the car onto a soft shoulder of dust and stones. "What's the matter?"

"I saw something in that car lot."

"What?" his father said, appearing a little annoyed.

"Just go back, okay?"

When it was safe his father made a U-turn, then drove about one hundred yards before veering into a dirt parking lot. A cloud of dust swirled around them as they came to a stop. And that's when Stony saw it, Leopold and Abraham's old Taurus, squatting between a red pickup truck and a rusting blue Chevy Blazer. Twenty or thirty other clunkers were scattered around.

"Damn," his father said, getting out of the Highlander and walking toward the Taurus.

Stony didn't say anything as he circled the station wagon with his father. They drew nearer, inspecting its insides. All of Leopold's and Abraham's belongings had been removed, and the old leather seats had been scrubbed clean. Stony was about to open the door when he heard a voice behind him say, "I worked on it all morning."

Stony turned and saw a flabby man in baggy jeans and a grease-stained white T-shirt. His head was shaved, but he had a long brown beard that descended into a point he had fashioned into a perverse braid. His teeth were yellow, and a penny-sized wart, like a third eye, sprouted from the center of his forehead. It was reddish and raw, threatening to explode. In spite of his grotesque appearance, he seemed happy.

"The name's Jody," he said, offering his hand to Stony's father, who shook it. "You interested in this car?"

"Very interested," Stony said.

"It looks weird from the outside, don't it? But it's got a strong engine and it cleaned up nice."

"We don't want to buy it," Stony's father said. "We want to know where the guys are who sold it to you."

"Are you a cop or something? Because I run a straight-up place."

"No," his father said. "We know these guys."

Jody scrutinized them. "I can't see you being buddies with those animals."

"Why do you call them animals?" Stony asked.

"I'm sixty-three years old, son, and I've had this place since I was twenty-five. I've seen a lot of oddballs and tough guys, but that skinny one gave me the creeps. If he'd been alive at Day One, he'd a been kicked out of Eden before Adam and Eve. I was ready to give him twenty-five bucks just to leave."

"So you don't know where they are?" Stony's father asked.

"They came in yesterday at about six, and after they got their money, they grabbed their backpacks and hiked into the woods." He pointed to a pine-covered hill that dwarfed his barn.

"Where exactly?" Stony asked.

"Right up that little mountain. It was like they burrowed through the center of it."

"With just backpacks?"

"They had all kinds of gadgets and pans attached to the packs. These guys looked like they could live up there until winter."

"What about the stuff that was in the car?"

"It was junk," Jody said. "Today's garbage day, so it got carted away a few hours ago. The only thing left is that," he added, pointing to a grill lying on its side near the garage. "I thought I might fix it up." He paused, then asked if he could get Stony and his father a Coke.

"No, we're fine."

"You guys have a beef with those two?"

"You could say that," Stony's father said.

"Well, I wouldn't worry about it. They said they were heading to Maine, and when I told them they'd have an easier time on the interstate, the skinny one said there wouldn't be much to feed on going that way. Kind of gave me the willies, but in a way, he's right. If you know the woods, you can take care of yourself, though they had enough money to buy food and another car. When I paid him, he opened an old leather billfold, stuffed with cash. If I had that kind of dough, I would've been holed up at the Ramada Inn, watching ESPN on one of those big-ass flat-screen TVs." He laughed loudly. "Sure you don't want a Coke? I got Diet Coke, too."

"No, but thanks," Stony's father said. "Do you mind if we look inside the car before we leave? I know that sounds weird, but I have my reasons."

"I don't have to know nothin'," Jody said, "but if you need a second car, you know where to go." He turned and shuffled off to the barn, every once in a while chuckling to himself.

After he left, Stony sat in the passenger-side seat and opened the glove compartment, expecting a disembodied hand to fall onto the floor. He looked through the windshield, thinking of how Leopold had stared through this same window while trying to run them off the road. He thought of the other people who had occupied this seat, and of what crimes they and Leopold had committed. He searched the glove compartment, but all he found were grains of tobacco. Meanwhile, his father was looking under the seats.

"Old Jody didn't leave much for us."

"What are we looking for?" Stony asked.

"I don't know," his father said, moving to the back of the car, where again they discovered nothing.

"You know, it's all obvious," Stony said.

"I know where you're going with this."

"Where else is there to go? You don't really think this is a coincidence."

"What I think is these yahoos never had an idea where they were going, so they kept driving and ended up here because it was a place Sally mentioned. And you heard Jody. By now they're on their way to Maine. Look, I'll be the first to say this is weird, but it's over," Stony's father said.

"You don't think we should call the police?"

"Do you know how nutty we'd sound?"

Stony had to agree. Outside of his theories, they

had no proof of anything, and what cop was going to scour the woods for two creeps who really hadn't done anything but intimidate them?

"One thing," his father said. "We don't say anything to Sally or Molly."

"Don't you think we should warn them?"

His father hesitated. "Not if we don't physically see these guys again. If that happens, I plan to finish it myself, anyway."

Stony closed the hatch on the Taurus, and they both returned to the Highlander, his father stopping to survey the surrounding mountains.

"You think they're up there, don't you?" Stony said.

"You watch too many movies."

"I hope you're right."

His father started the Highlander and was about to pull away when Jody galloped out of the barn waving a piece of paper. "Whoa there," he called.

Stony opened his window.

Jody was out of breath by the time he reached the car. "I forgot one thing. It's kind of dirty," he said to Stony's father, "so I don't know if the boy should see it, but they left this behind in the glove compartment."

Stony grabbed it. It was a napkin with a very realistic drawing of two women, one young and one middle-aged, standing at the counter of a McDonald's. The two women were laughing, posed provocatively and wearing no clothes. Their breasts were exaggerated, and the artist had drawn a grotesque flying creature over them. At first Stony didn't make the connection, but then he noticed the cut of Molly's hair and the outline of Sally's features. He felt embarrassed and angry at the same time.

"What is it?" Stony's father said.

"Nothing," he said. "Let's just get out of here."

But his father snatched the napkin and stared at the drawing. Then he crumpled it up and handed it back to Jody, saying, "Throw it away."

"How many shirts you going to try on?" Molly said. She was stretched out on a twin bed, still in her clothes from the Polar Caves, though she had removed her boots. She was reading a novel, lying on her stomach, propped up on her elbows with her ankles crossed. The bedroom she and Stony shared was furnished with two twin beds. Sally and their father occupied the master bedroom across the hall, which had a king-sized bed with a fairly large bathroom. Stony's and Molly's bathroom was smaller, but the shower was strong, and that was all Stony cared about.

"What are you reading?" he asked, finally settling on a dark brown T-shirt.

She smiled. "All that posing for *that* shirt?"

"Gimme a break, Princess," he said.

"If you call me that again, I'll break your nose."

"So who is it? Austen?"

"It's *Tess of the D'Urbervilles* by Thomas Hardy."

"Is it good?"

"A little creepy, but I like the main character. I want things to work out for her, but one of my friends said it doesn't. It's weird reading a book when you know that. I'm at a section called 'The Woman Pays,' which doesn't inspire a lot of confidence. But *you'd* like it. A lot of bad guys in it."

Her comment made Stony think of Leopold. He wanted to tell Molly about the Taurus, but he had promised. He also remembered how freaked out she'd been on the interstate.

"Can I come with you?" she asked.

"You're kidding, right?"

"I promise to say hi and leave."

"Fat chance."

"I noticed you're taking your suit and a towel. Does that mean a midnight swim somewhere?"

She was looking into her book, but Stony could see her smiling, so he didn't answer. Instead, he studied himself in a cheap, full-length mirror attached to the inside of a closet door. He looked pretty good—brown seersucker shorts, brown leather sandals, and the dark brown T-shirt. It fit snugly, and he was glad he'd been lifting weights. His father was probably right about him being handsome, but it wasn't something he thought about. In a way he looked like all the other blond-haired, blue-eyed kids at school, except he had an unusually broad, square jaw that gave a hard edge to his appearance. He was looking forward to seeing Ruth, but he could feel a sore throat coming on, beginning as a tickle and now a continuous burn.

"Listen to this," Molly said, reading a passage about a threshing machine and Tess's reaction to it. Stony didn't know the story, but it was a powerful scene. "I'll bet no one writes like that in your books," she said.

He wrapped the towel around his bathing suit and wedged it in under his arm. "That's because they're not novels. They're psychosocial studies."

"Don't make me giggle," Molly said.

"What are you guys doing tonight?"

"Just hanging around and playing some Uno. You know, I really like Sally. Sometimes I feel bad about it."

"Why?"

"Like I'm betraying Mom."

"But Mom likes her."

"I know, but I wonder what it's like to be part of a normal family."

"There isn't any such thing."

Molly closed her book and sat up. "You really believe that?"

"Think about your friends and tell me who has a normal life."

"Is this a homework assignment?"

"You bet."

"Okay, as long as you tell me if you get to first base."

Stony laughed. "I thought that line died forty years ago." He tapped her on the side of her head and left the bedroom, looking for Sally and his father on the way out of the condo, but they had gone for a walk. Suddenly he felt nervous. He wondered if Ruth would show up.

When he entered the office, the receptionist he'd spoken with the previous night winked at him, saying Ruth was downstairs. The wink was corny, but he knew she was trying to be nice.

He found Ruth playing an ancient Pac-Man video game, her back to him. She was wearing a tight white top, pink mid-thigh shorts, and pink flip-flops. Her hair had been washed and dried. It was evenly cut to shoulder length, and it glowed, seeming to absorb the energy of the indoor lighting; it pitched from side to side every time she shook the machine. There were two boys about ten years old playing pinball next to her, but no one was using the Ping-Pong table in the center of the room; two unused paddles rested on either side of the net, one smothering an orange ball.

Stony decided to hang back and admire Ruth as she wrestled with the machine. She appeared to be losing and not very happy about it. When he finally risked interrupting her, she said, "Do you like what you see?" never glancing away from the screen and continuing to manipulate the joystick. "The screen's like a mirror, Stony. If you want to stalk someone, you have to be more careful."

Stony anticipated a short evening after that comment, but when the game ended she grabbed his arm and smiled. "Actually I'm flattered." She had brushed mascara on her eyelashes and glossed her lips, so she looked about four years older than she had the night before. As Stony inspected this older-looking Ruth and inhaled her perfume, he felt there'd been some mistake, that someone as beautiful and smart and witty as her should've been waiting for someone older than him. She scrutinized him, then focused on the towel under his arm. "Good, you brought your suit."

They played Pac-Man for a while, not saying much. Later, she challenged him to Ping-Pong. He won the first two games, then let her win the third, making the match as close as possible.

"Where did you learn to play so well?" she asked. "I usually always win."

"My father's big on games. He'll pitch pennies if there's nothing else to do."

"I bet he usually wins."

"Most of the time, but he brings out the best in me."

"Why?"

"Because when he's a jerk I play harder."

After Ping-Pong they went for a swim. Everyone had left for the night, so they had the pool to themselves. Stony was a bit disappointed that Ruth had decided to wear a one-piece Speedo. When he dove into the cold water he felt his whole body erupt with goose bumps, his muscles cramping until he came to the surface. They swam together off and on for about a half hour, never touching, just moving from one end of the pool to the other, making small talk about school. There was a clock over the entrance to the pool, and Stony periodically checked it, knowing they had to be out by nine. There were no coffee shops or restaurants in walking distance, no place to take Ruth, and he didn't want the night to end.

At about ten to nine, she asked him back to her condo for a snack. They were sitting on lounge chairs with their towels wrapped around their shoulders. She was wiping mascara from her eyes with a tissue.

"Shouldn't you ask your mother?"

Ruth laughed. "She won't be home until after midnight. She met some guy hiking yesterday, and he's taking her to a concert in Waterville Valley."

"Cool," he said.

"Yeah, if you want to hear a sixty-year-old rock star play the one song that made him famous."

Stony didn't know what to say.

"My mother's specialty is guys in their mid-fifties who are happy to wine and dine any forty-year-old who's pretty. By the time they're that old, they're usually well off, so my mother keeps thinking one of them will marry her, put us up in a big house, and send me to private school. The problem, though, is that they have a lot of forty-year-old women to choose from."

"You make her sound promiscuous."

She looked startled. "Did you really say that?"

Stony would gladly have taken it back.

"Next you'll be talking about chastity belts. None

of those concepts work anymore. No, she's not *promiscuous*. She's just lonely, which of course is pathetic, but she does love me. The good news is she won't be home until late, so we have the whole condo to ourselves, but if you get fresh, I'll knock your head off."

Ruth's condo had the same layout as Stony's. You entered into a large living room separated from the kitchen by a fireplace. Ruth told Stony to sit while she got some "goodies" from the kitchen. He plopped down in a recliner and grabbed the TV remote from an end table. "Do you mind if I put on the television?" he asked.

"Yeah, I do."

He set down the control and stood, then wandered toward sliding glass doors that opened onto an enclosed patio, which overlooked a ravine. Although it was evening, light from the other condos made it possible to see bats crazily crisscrossing the sky. Gazing out into the darkness, he wondered what Leopold and Abraham were doing tonight—probably dining on some poor unsuspecting beaver or making stew from dead beetles and the heads of toads. Thinking of the drawing Jody gave him, he became concerned for Molly and Sally, but that thought was pleasantly disrupted by the presence of Ruth leaning slightly against him. He was surprised when he felt her head against his shoulder, and he almost turned to kiss her.

As if knowing his intention, she slid away and went back to the kitchen, where she had filled a bowl with taco chips and poured two glasses of Coke. When she returned, she asked him to join her on the couch. "Let's just talk for a while," she said. "Have some *real* conversation."

"*Real* conversation?"

"Yeah, like why did your father say you were angry and read books about whack jobs? You're about as scary as Scooby-Doo."

Stony laughed.

"You're not going to cut me up into little pieces, are you?" she said, handing Stony his Coke.

"I don't see why reading about the Kennedy assassination makes me weird," he said.

"Well, it's not your usual hobby, like stamp collecting or astronomy."

"I guess I've just spent more time thinking about why people do lousy things to each other. I know that's boring to most people, but it's important to me."

"It's worse than boring. It's depressing. Why don't you just go to church and light a candle?"

"Don't tell me you're never scared by what people are capable of."

Ruth frowned. "Well, there's one thing I worry about. Do you ever wake up in the middle of the night with the creeps?"

"The 'creeps'?"

"Like you're all alone, and your stomach feels hollow. That's when I pray, because I'm afraid if I close my eyes I won't exist anymore. It will all have been a big stupid dream."

Stony wanted to tell her he had the creeps most nights, but instead he sat quietly until he surprised himself by saying, "My grandmother was murdered when I was about eleven." Then he told her the whole story, finishing by confiding that he hadn't felt like himself since the murder.

"I'm sorry," Ruth said. "It makes sense now."

"What?"

"Why you read those books."

"I'm convinced there are evil people out there, people who have done so many terrible things they're not human, and I think we all carry that evil inside us, but for some reason most of us are too decent to give in to it."

"You really think everyone is evil."

"I'm not saying that, but after the murder I felt something rancid hanging around, and I waited every day for someone else to pick up a hammer or knife." He looked at her. All her makeup had been washed off, but she was still beautiful.

"Did you go into therapy?"

"Oh yeah."

"I've done that too," she said.

"What for?"

"They say I have 'intimacy issues.'"

Stony laughed.

"No, it's true."

"So did they cure you?"

She looked annoyed. "I guess I shouldn't have started this conversation," she said, leaning over the end table and grabbing the remote. The television came to life in the middle of a *CSI Miami* episode. "Not exactly the best program right now," she said, changing to the Cartoon Network, where Tom and Jerry were battling it out. She muted the volume and dimmed the lights. She started to kiss him but then backed off, saying, "You should go."

"Did I do anything wrong?" he asked.

She seemed nervous. "No, I just need to be alone, okay?" She paused, then added, "Just promise not to be mad at me in the morning."

"Why would I be mad?"

She didn't answer. Instead, she kissed him on the

forehead and ushered him to the door. When he turned to say goodbye, he noticed a few tears on her cheeks.

Molly was sound asleep by the time he wandered home, *Tess of the D'Urbervilles* resting upside down on her pillow. He placed it in the same position on the dresser so she wouldn't lose her place. Then he peeked outside the doorway and saw TV light bleeding from the bottom of his father's and Sally's bedroom door. He retreated and fell fully clothed on top of his bed. The drapes were open and a full moon bathed the room in silver. He felt a bit stunned, trying to make sense of his time with Ruth, trying to guess why she cried.

Later, lying in bed, shirtless and in pajama bottoms, and unable to sleep, he got up and looked out the window as a motorcycle pulled into the parking lot. An older man and his young girlfriend shared its seat. They were drunk and arguing, saying vile things to each other. Someone yelled for them to shut up, and they did. He could hear cars migrating down the interstate in the distance, then every once in a while the roar of a tractor-trailer drowning out crickets, and finally an odd noise, a scrounging or clawing, like a bear foraging through one of the dumpsters. He scanned the parking lot but didn't see anything, just lights from TVs streaming out condo windows.

Leopold adjusted the binoculars, focusing on the blond man and boy, who, unknowingly, were looking directly at them, and that was the fun part, to be seen yet unseen, imagining himself in the blond man's skin, feeling the fear of being tracked, "sized up for dinner," his father used to say, and it was clear the end was near, though delayed because of that boy on the road, because they had to ditch the car and change the plan, but now they knew where the blond man was staying, so take the day to hunt and gather and wait for a vehicle to present itself, which it did that night—a fat, bearded man, "He could be your brother, Abraham," stumbling out of a country bar, dumb enough to offer them a ride to a cottage that never existed, this second kill priming him for the final one, the light-versus-darkness one, the dream of falling come true, and later, he'd park the dead man's truck in an unused lot and hike a few hundred yards through the woods, sitting in darkness across from the lit windows, waiting for the outlines of the blond man or boy or two women, wondering what they were doing their last full day on earth, and to pass the time he whittled twigs into miniature arrows with a hunting knife until all the lights went off, just about to leave when he saw the boy walking across the parking lot and entering the condominium, and he took a chance moving into the artificial light, crouching behind a dumpster, as a motorcycle pulled up and stopped, a man and woman yelling at each other, then going into the same building as the boy, who suddenly appeared in a window, his bare chest illuminated by outdoor lights, Leopold, so taken by his nakedness, he stumbled, scraping his knife against the dumpster, the boy shifting his gaze but seeing nothing.

Stony woke to bright sunlight. He hadn't brushed his teeth, and could feel remnants of taco chips wedged between his teeth. His sore throat was worse and he felt feverish. He rolled away from the brightness, noticing that Molly had already made her bed. The bedroom door was closed, though he could hear people moving about in the kitchen. It was eight o'clock. His father had wanted to reach Castle in the Clouds by nine, so he was surprised no one had roused him.

He got up and stretched out his back and hamstrings. Still groggy, he wandered into the bathroom, where he dampened a facecloth and rubbed his face. Then he brushed his teeth. When he finished, he put on a T-shirt and headed toward the kitchen. His father, Sally, and Molly sat behind a white Formica counter, munching on Cheerios and orange slices and sipping coffee from cheap white mugs that came with the condo. He waited for the ribbing to begin.

"Hi, sleepyhead," Molly said.

Stony stared dumbly at them.

"What?" his father said.

"I'm waiting for the inquisition."

"Why would we 'inquisit' you?" his father said, working to suppress a smile.

At that, Sally elbowed his father, and Molly lowered her spoon, saying, "Sally said if we razz you, she'll get us lost in the woods and leave us there."

Stony turned his attention to Sally, who sat on a stool at the end of the counter. She had an endless supply of interchangeable T-shirts and hiking shorts, today's color being dark brown, which matched her thick socks, one of which wasn't completely pulled up, revealing what looked like a black Ace bandage. Sally noticed him staring at it.

"It's a knife," she said.

"A knife?"

She walked into the kitchen and poured Stony a glass of orange juice. He took a sip, the acidic pulp burning the back of his throat. "A small Swiss Army knife," she said. She slid her sock down, now fully displaying a black wrap with a little pocket that housed the knife. "You should never be in the woods without a knife."

"What a woman," his father said. "She's been up

all morning making lunches and packing enough insect repellent to nuke a horde of mutant mosquitoes."

"You won't be laughing when we're in the woods," Sally said.

"You're not spraying me with that stuff. Bugs never bother me."

"We'll see."

It was clear everyone had been waiting for him, and his father said, "Now that you're up, Stony, could you hurry so we're the first ones there?"

"Take your time," Sally said. "We have to pack the car. I'll leave the cereal on the counter."

Stony nodded and drifted back to the bedroom. There, he stripped and stepped into the shower, thinking he could still smell Ruth's perfume on him.

The plan was to reach Castle in the Clouds early and to hike a few hours before visiting the mansion itself. On the way there, Molly, who had become their unofficial tour guide, gave them a brief history of its owner, reading from a pamphlet. "Castle in the Clouds," she said, speaking in a mock-formal tone, "was built in the early nineteen hundreds by industrialist Thomas Plant, who called it Lucknow. He had the top of the mountain leveled and used the rock to construct his house. He employed one thousand workers, mostly Italian stonemasons from Boston, but also carpenters and teamsters. It has a southern exposure and is built on a solid ledge foundation of local pink granite. The house has Maine oak beams, hand hewn in a Bath shipyard. Recessed cement gives the appearance of seamless construction of the pentagonal stonework. The roof is of Spanish tile."

"Okay, I get the picture," Stony's father interrupted.

Molly smirked, then continued. "Plant had a hydro-generator installed in the stables. An outside fire hydrant, with hose and connectors on each floor of the mansion, attests to Plant's concern about fire. Plant also maintained a farm on the highway, producing beef, pork, and lamb." She stopped to take a breath.

"Didn't I read he was a real whack job?" Stony's father said.

"I think 'eccentric' is the word you're looking for," Sally said.

"Which is a fancy word for whack job," his father replied.

"Supposedly," Molly added, "he was an innovator. In one of his plants he had people wear roller skates, making it easy for them to move around."

"And for him to make more money."

"Dad's right," Stony said.

"Finally, he has awakened," his father said.

"Yeah, why so quiet this morning?" Molly asked.

"Actually, I'm not feeling well."

"I have some aspirin," Sally said.

"No, it's just a sore throat. But getting worse."

At the entrance to Castle in the Clouds they stopped at an information kiosk, where they were given a map of the grounds and hiking trails. They were told that halfway up the mountain was a little waterfall, and then a little farther, a promontory overlooking Lake Winnipesaukee and most of the Ossipee mountain range.

The drive was more of an adventure than Stony had anticipated, up a steep paved road with nothing but small saplings between them and a gorge. As the car climbed higher the pine trees became larger and denser. Finally they pulled into a little dirt parking lot and walked about half a mile to the waterfall, where they took pictures and soaked their feet in a freezing clear pool fed by the falls. After drying off, they continued to the promontory. It was more humid than on the previous day, but the sky was clear and visibility endless. Growing up in a city, Stony had never seen anything like this. Below him, Lake Winnipesaukee spread out and curled through the mountains like an enormous swollen river. Dwarfing the lake, different levels of gray-shaded ranges and peaks vied for attention. It was as if God, like a little kid playing at the beach, had gouged out and molded the landscape, then nourished the cavities with water from a huge celestial pail.

"Damn," his father said.

"Damn," Stony repeated.

"And this is just the beginning," Sally said. "Our hike takes us to a spot called Bald Knob, where it's even prettier."

"It almost makes you woozy," Molly said.

Invigorated, they returned to the Highlander and started up the narrow road again. Finally they reached a parking lot on top of a hill that overlooked a small vale.

Before Stony's father could shut down the engine, Sally told him to park at the bottom of the hill. She pointed toward a pond and two wooden structures, saying, "There're supposed to be trout swimming there. After we hike and eat, we can shower and freshen up in the restrooms, then go to the mansion." She had told everyone to pack a change of clothes, and she had placed protein bars and bottles of water in their small backpacks.

At the bottom of the hill Stony's father parked near some picnic tables. He opened the hatch and placed their cooler on one of them. "I doubt anyone will steal it."

"I don't know," Stony said. "If someone's shooting hitchhikers, stealing a little food won't rock their worlds."

"Another inspirational message from the eternal optimist," his father said. Then he pointed to the pond. "Let's check that out."

The pond wasn't more than fifty yards in diameter but was stocked with huge trout, along with ducks, who fought them for food. A boardwalk rimming the pond supported three machines that for a quarter spit out a handful of brown pellets. Stony and Molly tossed them into the air, watching the larger trout break the surface to snatch them.

After about fifteen minutes of this feeding frenzy, Sally led them to a service road about fifty yards away. Stony's father said, disappointed, "This ain't exactly roughing it."

Sally studied the trail map. The service road led to trails that would eventually take them twenty-five hundred feet above sea level, Sally said. They'd snack there and take a few pictures.

About a quarter of a mile into the hike, Stony began to attract mosquitoes, which he swatted. "Can I have some repellent?" he asked.

"Shoot," Sally said. "That was my job. I left it in the car."

"I'll go back," Stony said.

"Not necessary," his father said. "I told you, mosquitoes don't like me."

"Well, they like *me*," Sally said.

"And me too," Molly seconded.

"Okay," Stony's father said, tossing Stony the keys.

"The repellent's on the floor where I was sitting," Sally said.

Stony left his pack with Molly and jogged back toward the pond. By now, there was another vehicle, an old blue pickup, parked twenty-five yards from their car. Stony opened the Highlander and grabbed the insect repellent, then closed the door and pressed the lock button on the keychain. By the time he rejoined his family, they were standing at the opening of a well-groomed trail that branched off the service road. "Well, if it isn't Apollo Ohno," his father joked. Stony handed Sally the repellent, and she sprayed everyone from head to toe.

"Not me," his father said.

"Don't be an ass, Arthur."

"I'm serious. That stuff's poisonous."

"This isn't the city. They'll eat you up."

"Not if we keep moving," he said, challenging everyone to follow him.

"Slow down?" Sally said. "It would be nice if the kids got to see a few birds along the way."

"There're enough birds in the city."

Sally groaned, and hearing it, Stony's father slackened his pace. Meanwhile Stony saw Sally remove a thick yellow crayon from her pack and jam it into the front pocket of her shorts. He wondered if she planned on jotting down their names on some huge granite boulder when they reached the top.

For half an hour they weaved their way through a pine forest infiltrated by scrub-oak thickets. Some of the pines were old and healthy and huge, some seemed younger, and still others appeared ready to die, coated with scabs of moss and lichen. At one point Sally pushed over the stump of a scaly tree, explaining that its roots, now dead, could no longer grip the sandy ground. "It's a disease called *Armillaria*," Sally said, "and it can kill trees already weakened by pests or storms." Even

Stony's father seemed interested as she spoke about the vegetation and animal life in the White Mountains, though it seemed as if they had scared off every living creature.

Finally they arrived at a little stream, which Stony's father wanted to follow upward, even though the groomed trail led elsewhere.

"We should stay on the trail," Sally said. She looked at Molly, who was wearing a blue cotton top with thin straps. "I don't want her getting scratched. I'm also worried about ticks."

Stony's father pointed to a spot ten yards upstream. "That looks like an old trail. Don't you think it'd be more fun hiking by a stream?"

Stony thought it looked like a trail, too, and it seemed wide enough to accommodate them.

Sally hesitated. "Okay, but if the trail gets difficult, I want to backtrack."

"Sure," his father said, squashing a mosquito sucking blood from his forearm.

Sally removed the repellent from her backpack, but Stony's father waved her off. "Don't you think it's awfully quiet here?" he said.

"That's the point," she said.

They followed the new trail along the river for about fifteen minutes before it ended. Unused to woods, Stony felt hemmed in, unable to see anything but pines and boulders, and the ground felt unnaturally soft underfoot. "Are we lost?" he asked.

"We just have to follow the stream back down. It will lead to the trail," Sally said.

Stony's father, by now measled by mosquito bites, urged everyone to keep moving.

"You promised," Sally said.

He pointed to the left and above. "That looks like another trail, and it leads up. Isn't that the point, to get to the top? Once we're there, we can choose the best route back."

"It isn't that simple, Arthur."

But Stony's father was already on the move.

"I'm getting a little tired," Molly said.

"We'll be there soon," Sally said, massaging Molly's shoulders. "It can't be more than fifteen or twenty minutes."

"Follow the leader," his father said, pushing aside bushes and twigs.

There were more than just pine trees now. Large shrubs and twigs and bushes closed in around them, scraping the flesh of a leg or an arm. Stony felt his breath quicken, and he didn't want to stop for fear of being eaten alive by a bear, the forest, or even the faint mist that suddenly descended on them. After fifteen more minutes of vigorous hiking, they reached a clearing encircled by pines, its floor soft with needles.

"Finally," his father said.

"Finally what?" Sally asked.

His father didn't know what to say, because she was right. They had indeed reached an opening, but they were far from the top, and when Stony looked behind, the trail seemed to have vanished.

"I'm scared," Molly said.

"Don't worry," Sally said. "I have this covered."

"Say what?" Stony's father asked.

Sally held up her yellow crayon. "I've been marking trees."

Stony's father's laugh echoed loudly through the forest. He hugged Sally and kissed her on the lips. "What a woman!"

Stony had been feeling sicker by the moment and was now dizzy and weak-kneed, but he didn't want to complain and ruin the hike. "Do you hear that?" he asked.

"What?" Molly said.

"I think it's that stream. Maybe if it's nearby we can take a dip."

"Don't go far, Stony," Sally said, giving him the crayon. "Mark a tree every five or ten yards. Meanwhile, the rest of us can have a snack."

"Sounds like a plan," Stony's father said, suddenly happy he hadn't gotten them lost and killed off by the elements.

Stony left the group and pushed through the trees, leaving large yellow X's behind him. Finally, downhill, about sixty feet away, he saw the stream, branching off in three directions like the tongs of a bent fork. One of the branches emptied into a shallow pool. He drifted there, wanting to refresh himself and soak his kerchief. He didn't know if it was the heat or his worsening sore throat, but he was on fire—the trees, foliage, even the exposed tree roots trembling in the dusty sunlight.

When he reached the pool he knelt on a large flat rock, dipping the kerchief into the cold water and wringing it out. Suddenly a shrill screech tore through the air, and he looked up, thinking he'd see a hawk bearing down on him, but there was nothing. He retied the kerchief around his brow. The pool was fairly still; tiny water spiders crisscrossed each other's paths.

As he cupped water, his reflection appeared, and then another face, a head much larger and rounder than his and also wearing a kerchief. Before he could confront this doppelganger, he took a blow to the temple. His mouth filled with cool stream water before he lost consciousness.

He awoke unable to move his limbs. His vision was blurred, his head hurt from the blow, and he could taste snot. His throat was still sore and dry, as if he'd been sleeping with his mouth open. Slowly the surroundings came into focus. Directly across from him, not more than twenty feet away, his father was strapped with duct tape to a huge pine tree. Stony himself was anchored to another pine. Straining to look upward, he noticed that his tree ended a few feet above his head. The remainder of it lay nearby, probably felled by a bolt of lightning years before. He couldn't see Molly or Sally, or Leopold and Abraham, though the latter two had done a good job. His wrists were bound tight, and he and his father had been fastened in three places: the shins, waist, and chest. The tape around his upper body was so tight he could hardly breathe, though at least he could talk, unlike his father, whose mouth was taped shut. Stony wondered how they had managed to secure his father, imagining him fighting until he was completely spent, even though he wasn't bruised or bloody. Still, his face was a mess, as were his arms and legs. The mosquito bites he'd gotten earlier were blossoming.

Stony heard voices to his left and saw Leopold and Abraham leading Sally and Molly toward them. When Sally noticed that Stony was conscious, she tried to approach him, but Abraham pushed her and Molly onto the ground.

"You all right?" Sally asked.

Stony nodded, then looked at Molly. Her blue cotton top was damp with sweat and clinging to her small breasts. She had been crying and was trembling, holding her arms around her knees, rocking back and forth, unable to take her eyes off the ground, as if thinking Leopold and Abraham might vanish if she didn't look up.

Leopold stood in front of Stony, so close their faces almost touched. He hadn't shaved for a few days, and his hair reeked of dead leaves and dirt; his breath was putrid, and a purplish welt stained his left cheek. Stony stared into his eyes, refusing to look away until Leopold spit in his face, saying, "Like father, like son."

"Ain't it the truth," Abraham said.

Stony's father tried to free himself, groaning fiercely, his face suffused with anger.

"Did they hurt you?" Stony asked Molly and Sally.

Sally looked away. Neither Sally's nor Molly's clothes had been torn, but Sally's expression seemed distant. Her complexion, which yesterday had been ruddy from sun and exercise, was now pale, her lower lip bruised, her hands and knees soiled with mud.

"Why would we hurt them, Stony?" Leopold said. He wore a sweat-soaked black T-shirt and black sweat pants that had been cut off at the shins. The handle of a gun protruded from the waistband. Now Stony understood why his father hadn't fought back. Which was a mistake. Better to be shot on the spot, Stony thought, than to be duct-taped to trees and tortured.

He could feel Leopold's spit drying on his cheek and he wanted to vomit. His father continued to struggle with the tape, Leopold watching him, slowly pacing back and forth. Finally, he stopped in front of Stony's father and slapped him hard in the face.

"Stop it," Sally yelled.

"Just trying to kill that mosquito," Leopold said. "King Arthur's going to be one sorry mess tomorrow."

"Ain't it the truth," Abraham said. He wore a dirty white T-shirt and old blue overalls, and he was barefoot.

Leopold slapped Stony's father again. "Dang, I got another one."

"Let me help," Abraham said, striking him with the back of his hand. "That should keep those varmints away." A slight wound opened over his father's left cheekbone.

Molly started to whimper but still didn't look up.

"At least let him breathe," Stony said.

Leopold examined Stony's father. "The man just wouldn't shut up. Wanted to ask a lot of questions. How did we find you? And then the usual, 'Just kill me. There's no reason to hurt them.'" Leopold looked at Abraham, who laughed, and then continued, "All we had to do was drive around until we spotted your car. You people make it easy because you talk too much, telling that hag at your fancy condo where you were going. Then it was just steal a truck and follow you. When we saw your big car parked near the trail I said to Abraham, 'The Devil's done good today.'"

Sally looked up. "Haven't you gotten what you wanted?"

Leopold laughed. "You think I wanted *you*? I could've gotten that at the—" He looked at Abraham. "What was the name of that bar?"

"The Loon," Abraham said.

"Yeah, I could've gotten that at The Loon." He walked back to Stony's father and punched him in the stomach. "Why do you think we herded you away? I would've done King Arthur a favor by killing you." He went nose to nose with Stony's father. "But better to let King Arthur imagine it all, like he is now, dreaming about tearing Leopold's head off." He removed the gun from his waist and held the barrel to Stony's father's temple. "It'd be too easy to kill you. When you're dead the pain stops." He lowered the gun and replaced it in its makeshift holster, then moved even closer to Stony's father. "Leopold needs to have a little conversation with King Arthur, fill in some of the blanks."

He spoke softly into Stony's father's ear for about five minutes, his father's eyes periodically shifting toward Sally and Molly. When he finished, he told Abraham to give him Stony's kerchief, and he gently dabbed Stony's father's face. "I think the man's crying," he said. "Yes, I'm sure these are tears."

He crept over to two backpacks about ten feet away, emptying out more rolls of duct tape. He pointed to two pines, one not more than five feet from Stony. "Abraham, tape these two ladies to those trees over there," he said.

Abraham secured Sally but had trouble budging Molly. She had centered her weight into the earth, perhaps thinking she might grow roots and be left alone. Eventually Abraham made her stand, and he taped her to the other tree. When he was done, her head rested lifelessly on her chest. Meanwhile Abraham tore off her cuff bracelet, creating a bloody scratch. Molly never made a sound, never looked up. "A little souvenir," he said, holding it up to the sunlight.

"Now tape those two girls' mouths," Leopold said. He walked over to Sally and softly touched her lips with his middle finger. "Such a nice mouth," he said, smiling at Stony's father. "But we can't have any screaming."

Stony waited for them to gag him, but they didn't. Leopold moved toward him, and he braced himself for a slap or punch. "I don't like that nasty look, boy, but I know it. I think you and me ain't as different as you think. Maybe I came here for you. I always know there's a reason, but sometimes I don't see it till later."

"There's no reason for this," Stony heard himself say.

"What are you looking at, boy? My eye? Thank Abraham for that. After we kicked that tramp out of the car I sure hated myself for making a spectacle. Always better to stay low to the ground. My daddy once said, 'For every wrongdoing there must be punishment,' so I told Abraham to hit me, and, as you can see," he said, fingering the welt, "he gladly obliged. But I asked you, boy, what are you looking at?"

Stony didn't respond, so Abraham poked him hard in the ribs. "He asked you a question."

"No reason to hurt this boy," Leopold said. "Look at those eyes, Abraham, so filled with hate."

There was so much Stony wanted to say, but he couldn't get his mouth to work. He longed for a sound, any sound, to replace Abraham's wheezing. Distant traffic or even the faint cry of a loon would do. But nothing. The birds had stopped singing and the pine cones hung like icicles. Looking at the handle of Leopold's gun, Stony made a connection, and this time words came out. "You killed that kid, didn't you?"

Leopold smiled. "Killed? No, there was no killing. There was crime and there was punishment."

"They said he was killed in cold blood."

"They always say that, but there's no such thing. You die when it's time. I've been gifted to see death, behold it, like a big black halo floating over your head. Fact is me and Abraham is driving quietly down the road, and this boy's hitchhiking, so we stop the car, and when he reaches it, we drive away, then do it again. Everything would've been fine, just a little fun, but he has to give us the finger. No, that's not killing, me and Abraham call that retribution."

"Ain't it the truth," Abraham said, and he stood next to Stony. "Lookee here," he said, trying to pry Stony's grandfather's ring off his finger.

"It would be easier to cut the finger off," Leopold said.

Abraham nodded but gave the ring one more tug. It slipped from Stony's finger and fell to the ground. He snatched it and stuffed it into his front pocket.

"Bring the container, Abraham," Leopold said, and Abraham grabbed a red plastic jug from one of the bags. He tossed it to Leopold, who opened the top and, slowly circling Stony's family, emptied out its contents. "Time to tape that boy's mouth," Leopold said, and Abraham followed his orders.

Unable to breathe, Stony felt that his powers of smell were exaggerated and he could detect the odor of gasoline. When he struggled furiously to break free, Leopold came toward him and feinted a blow.

"No need to struggle, boy. We're near the end."

He and Abraham opened their backpacks and organized the contents in a very businesslike manner. Leopold unzipped a small pocket and withdrew a matchbox from it. He strapped on his pack, then scanned his victims, as if taking a mental snapshot of each one. When he removed a wooden match from the box, Stony's father rubbed his back violently against his tree.

Leopold shook his head. "It's a shame," he said. "All you had to do was eat your hamburgers and salads, but you stomped into my circle." He focused on Sally. "I wanted to tell you to walk away, but King Arthur wouldn't let that happen, and then he had to insult my momma, and I knew what I had to do."

He lit the match and tossed it toward a strip of gasoline-soaked pine needles. The flame turned end over end, taking an eternity to reach the ground. Just as it was about to land it died out. Leopold removed another match. "I'll give it two tries," he said. "If this one don't work, then I'll grant Him His victory and let you rot."

He lit another match and threw it high into the air. This time it landed while still on fire. Stony could have sworn he saw it ignite the gasoline, but it flamed out as if an invisible foot had trampled it. Leopold lifted his eyes to the heavens and laughed. He sidled up next to Stony, staring long and hard at him.

"Ain't we going to finish this?" Abraham asked.

"Let the bugs and critters eat 'em," Leopold said. "There's more than one way to kill a person."

Then he and Abraham secured them with more duct tape, gathered up the backpacks, and vanished. One moment they were in front of Stony; the next, all he saw was rocks and pine cones and fledgling trees. Maybe it was all a dream, he thought. Maybe I'll nod off, and when I wake up, nothing will have happened.

At first Stony couldn't open his eyes, the heat and dust having temporarily cemented his lids together. He had slept for about an hour, maybe two. His cold had settled into his sinuses, making it difficult to breathe. Finally able to focus, he noticed the sun's absence overhead and wondered how long it'd been since they entered the trail. They had hiked about forty-five minutes before they'd been attacked, and he guessed Leopold and Abraham had left somewhere around two p.m. Molly was sleeping. Sally and his father were struggling to free themselves. If he could have spoken, he would have told them to stop. They weren't the first victims Leopold and Abraham had taped to trees or poles or fences.

Still, Stony's father wouldn't quit, if the man twenty feet across from him was really his father. He looked like a corpse, his face swollen from bug bites, the cut from Abraham's blow still raw. Because Abraham had taken his hiking boots and socks, his feet were scratched and filthy from thrusting them again and again into the ground, trying to dislodge the huge pine. His T-shirt and shorts were stained with sweat, and mosquitoes continued to swarm around him. Helplessly watching him, Stony strained to uproot his own tree until he lost consciousness again.

While asleep he had a dream. From overhead, he was looking down on himself and the rest of his family, but there was also another figure, a man in a red flannel shirt and white overalls, methodically spading dirt from the base of Stony's tree. It was John, the handyman, but a different John from the one Stony had known. He was smiling, displaying a mouthful of perfect teeth, and his hair and beard were well groomed. Stony felt a rush of anger, but something in John's face disarmed him. This new John was about to speak until everything went white, as if a sheet had been placed over Stony's head.

It wasn't far from twilight when he awoke. He remembered the dream and was perplexed by it. Across from him his father was spent, as were Sally and Molly. A dark silence enveloped them, like the eerie quiet following a scream. Stony could only imagine how they looked to birds and trees and other wildlife; what odd, breathing statues they must have seemed.

Stony thought now that his hard thrusts before he passed out might have slightly budged the tree, so he began to struggle again. His tree was thinner than his father's, and he knew it must have been dead or dying. But even if he could uproot it, what would he be able to do? In between forward and backward lunges he looked at Sally, and that's when he saw it. From all her labor, her socks had slipped below her ankles, exposing the black wrap that held the Swiss Army knife. Leopold had missed it, too.

In quick bursts of rage and wild hope, Stony fought to free himself. The tree didn't move, but the sweat of his effort loosened the tape over his mouth. He pushed hard with his tongue until it fell to the ground, and then he spat out chunks of phlegm lodged in his throat. He breathed deeply, the air bringing energy to his limbs. This was his last chance before exhaustion and sickness won out. He battled savagely with the tree, howling at the sky. Molly watched him, and when Stony saw her pained expression, he yelled even louder, throwing his weight forward again and again until he found himself on the ground, the useless trunk still attached to his back.

It took some time, but he dragged himself toward Sally, positioning his hands by her feet. Despite the tape binding his hands together, he managed to grasp the knife and open it, shredding the tape around Sally's wrists. Freed, she took the knife from him. She slashed at the tape on herself and Stony, then ran toward Molly.

They were hurtling down the mountain with Sally in the lead. Behind her Stony's father followed barefoot, bearing Molly on his back, seemingly oblivious to the pine needles and pebbles and tangles of roots abusing his feet.

They were trusting in Sally's yellow marks, and that the forest would eventually end, that their punishment for cheating death wouldn't be to wander through thickets of vegetation forever. Now and then Molly would turn her head and search for Stony, afraid he might be left behind, and that stare made his head spin as he grasped vines and twigs for balance. When they reached the service road, they never stopped, never spoke until they entered the clearing and collapsed next to the Highlander.

There, his father grabbed a thin branch from under a tree and with Sally's knife whittled its end into a point, then used it like a screwdriver to pry off a hubcap and remove an extra key taped to its inside. He opened the back of the Highlander and tossed clothes onto the ground. Molly and Sally seemed so fixed on his actions that they didn't notice the cooler resting on the picnic table or the old blue truck fifty yards away. Leopold and Abraham had not come back.

When Stony spotted the cooler he ran to it and emptied its contents onto the ground. They all devoured sandwiches and gulped water or poured it onto their heads. Stony didn't want this feast to end, didn't want to face what came next. But Sally grabbed hold of Molly and some clothes and a bottle of wine she had brought and headed for the building where the restrooms and showers were.

"What are you doing?" Stony's father asked.

"We're going to shower," she said, as calmly as she might have said, *We're going for a walk.*

"You can't," he said. "You have to wait for the police."

"They'll never catch them," Sally said. She seemed strangely dispassionate, biting her lower lip.

"But we have to call them."

"I know what we're *supposed* to do, Arthur."

"What about Molly?"

"What do you want," Sally said, "to call the police and have them fix everything? You weren't there, so don't you dare tell me how to handle this. Maybe tomorrow or the next day, but not now."

Stony's father's hair was glued to his forehead, and he was spotted with mosquito bites. His feet were cut and bleeding. Stony had never seen him look so vulnerable.

"You don't get it, do you?" Molly said. "They hurt Sally and made me watch."

Hearing Molly, Stony remembered Leopold's words, *Better to imagine it.* That's what he had wanted, to hurt Sally and make Molly and his father play it back endlessly in their minds.

Stunned into silence, Stony's father fell to his knees. Sally placed the clothes and bottle of wine on the ground, then removed her first-aid kit from the back of the Highlander. She made him stand, then knelt next to him, working mechanically on his feet with a piece of gauze soaked in peroxide, trying to focus all her energy on one task.

"Don't," he said.

She ignored his comment and continued to clean his wounds.

Meanwhile, Stony gently held Molly. Although he was sitting there with people he knew to be his father and Sally and Molly, everyone seemed a stranger. Their old selves hadn't yet grasped how to respond to the day's unexpected cruelty.

"Sally," Stony finally said, "you and Molly can get cleaned up, and I'll take care of Dad."

But she refused to look up.

"Please," Stony pleaded.

She nodded, collected the wine and clothes and towels, and led Molly slowly toward the restrooms.

From the back of the Highlander, Stony grabbed clothes and soap and more towels and said, "Let's go, Dad," and his father allowed himself to be shepherded away.

The restrooms were constructed from planks of wood that had been stained red. The insides were spotless, except for a few spider webs occupying the corners of the ceiling. There were toilets to the right; to the left was the entrance to a shower room. Stony's father drifted to the left while Stony entered a stall and closed the door behind him. He fell to his knees and vomited phlegm into the toilet. His head still throbbed, though the lump over his right eye felt relatively small.

"You okay?" he heard his father ask. The door opened, and he stood in front of Stony wearing nothing but his dirt-stained hiking shorts. He looked dazed.

"I'm just sick."

His father nodded and left.

Stony locked the stall door, dropped his shorts, and sat on the toilet, emptying himself. He began to tremble inside. He sat quietly for a while, listening to the spray from his father's shower pepper the floor. When it stopped, more sounds came from the restroom next to theirs. Again the sound of showers, then Molly crying, and finally someone gargling. Above him a black spider, its body the size of a quarter, prowled its web. Stony finished his business, then opened the stall door. As he did, the spider lowered itself, menacingly. Stony stepped out of its path and chopped the thick filament spun from its belly, watching it collapse helplessly onto the floor and try to scurry away. But Stony was on it, grinding it into a plank with the toe of his boot.

He left the stall, moving toward a wounded, whimpering sound coming from the shower. There, his father sat naked on the wet concrete floor, crying into his lap. Stony sat next to him, locking his hands around his father's upper body, and surprisingly, his father didn't push him away. When Stony released his grip, his father wiped his eyes and said, "It's my fault."

"No, he wouldn't have stopped."

"But I took us off the path."

"If it hadn't been there, it would've been somewhere else."

"We have to do something."

"I know," Stony said.

He had never slept like normal people, instead drifting in and out of half dream states, heightened at times like these, seized by an animal intelligence until the killing was done, like a giant bug gnawing at his rib cage, burrowing its way out, and then a familiar exhaustion, afterward retreating alone into the woods, only to track down Abraham later, a ritual repeated until perfected, until he could shift in and out of real life as if invisible, as he was now, moving from rock to rock, slowing down time as he had learned to, Abraham lagging behind, then the boy drinking from a stream, forcing everything into action, Leopold no longer just bad ("That boy Leopold was born for trouble," his teachers had said), but something different, a world of hatred pulsing through him, so he watched Abraham do his business, watched with the young girl he hated, not knowing why she had to be hated, for thou will crawl on thy belly and eat dust for the rest of thy days, *but something different this time, seeing his fate in that boy's eyes, in the smell of sulfur, in the impossibility of a wooden match suffocated by a puddle of gasoline, then his gaze moving from tree to tree, resting on each taped face, unrecognizable now because of the suffering he too had once felt, until he and Abraham melted into a pool of dim light, thick with the beating of disembodied hearts—the ones he had set free.*

Stony wasn't going to fall asleep. He lay quietly on his bed, his knees drawn into his chest, watching two squirrels chase each other up a pine tree. His throat was so sore he could hardly swallow, and every muscle in his body ached. Molly was resting with Sally in the other bedroom, and he didn't know where his father was. In half an hour it would be dark.

On the way back from Castle in the Clouds, no one had spoken. Something had to be done, but everyone was waiting for Sally to decide what that something was. Stony had comforted Molly in the back seat, rubbing her back and periodically brushing the hair from her forehead. When they arrived at the condo, she went straight to the master bedroom with Sally while Stony and his father wiped down the back of the Highlander and arranged food in cupboards, doing anything physical to keep busy.

Stony needed to talk to someone, but he didn't want to leave Molly and Sally. He went to the living room and sat on a pullout couch, staring into the empty fireplace. Sally must have heard his movements, because she appeared in front of him, wearing a blue T-shirt and his father's red plaid pajama bottoms, the cuffs rolled up to mid-calf. Her hair was tied back, her face scrubbed clean. "You okay?" she asked.

"How can you worry about me?"

"Right now, I need to focus on you and your sister." She joined him on the couch, her chest making slight heaves. Leopold had stolen something from her in the woods, but she wasn't going to give in.

"We have to call the police," Stony said.

"I will, but not now. I know that's wrong, but there it is. They won't catch him anyway."

"How do you know?"

"Because he told me, and I believe him. He's the devil, Stony."

Stony remembered Leopold's eyes. "I know," he said, then looked toward the master bedroom, where Molly was.

"I gave her something to help her sleep," Sally said. She touched the lump on Stony's forehead, making him flinch. She got some ice from the freezer, wrapped a thin dish towel around it, and pressed it against the wound. "Hold it there for about fifteen minutes, okay?"

Stony nodded, and Sally returned to the bedroom.

He sat by himself for about ten minutes before leaving the condominium, at first walking aimlessly. Then he decided to pass by Ruth's and was surprised that all the lights were off. His fever had begun to affect his balance, but he made his way to the office. The gray-haired receptionist was about to close up.

"She's gone," the woman said.

"What?"

"They checked out," she said, then added, "What happened to your head?"

"I hurt it hiking."

"I'm sorry," she said. "I know you liked her."

He nodded, walking slowly toward the door. When he grasped the handle, the receptionist said, "There was a guy here this morning looking for your father, a strange little man, always glancing behind him and grinning like a chimpanzee. Did he find you?"

Yes, he found us, Stony thought, stumbling into the night. The sky was clear, brimming with stars, and a full moon cast shadows around him. As he crossed the road toward his condo, the wail from a horn froze him seconds before an SUV passed a few feet from his face.

Stony is back in Greece with Ianthe sipping from white ceramic espresso cups. They aren't speaking to each other, and that's fine. It's the quiet he wants. His eyes drift toward the horizon, taking in the quivering sails of tiny boats and a landscape so beautifully bathed in sunlight it seems inviolable. He wants to stay here forever, in the eternal present, but when he reaches for Ianthe's hand he hears . . .

"Stony, wake up."

His father was sitting on the edge of the bed. The bites on his face had calmed down, though the bruise over his eye still looked sore. He placed his hand on Stony's forehead. "Christ, you're burning up."

Stony forced himself awake. He shifted his eyes to Molly's bed, but she wasn't there.

"She's still sleeping with Sally," his father said.

"Where are you going?"

"I found that bar."

"What bar?"

"The one they talked about. The Loon. A guy working at a hardware store saw them a few hours ago. They must've figured we'd rot out there, that there was no hurry."

"Did you call the police?"

His father didn't answer.

"Did you hear me?" Stony asked again.

His father responded with, "Are you strong enough to come with me?"

Stony was hardly strong enough to sit, but he said yes. His father grabbed his arm, led him to the bathroom, and filled up the sink with cold water. He left the room and returned with palms full of ice that he emptied into the sink. "Stick your head in that for a few seconds."

Stony did as he was told, and when he surfaced, he felt more alert. He dried his face and hair with a white hand towel. "What time is it?"

"Not yet midnight. About eleven," his father said, handing him two aspirin, which he swallowed and washed down with handfuls of cold water.

"When are we leaving?"

"Shhhh, I don't want to wake them."

"Does Sally know what we're doing?"

His father ignored him.

"But she said she'd call the cops tomorrow," Stony said.

"It doesn't matter. They'd ask too many questions now, like why she waited."

Ten minutes later they were driving down a road unlit by streetlights. With the coming of night a mist had descended, hugging the ground, which itself was eerily illuminated by moonlight. Soon they turned onto a main drag leading toward town.

The alert sensation from Stony's impromptu baptism had faded, and his fever was back with a vengeance. Hardly able to breathe, he blew his nose every couple of minutes into a handkerchief. His father seemed to get the picture, so when they reached town he pulled into a little motel with tiny fishing cabins. "Wait here," he said. "I want you to be close if I need you."

He returned a few minutes later with a key and told Stony to follow him until they found themselves standing in the middle of a small cottage. There was one main room with two beds and an efficiency kitchen.

"Where's the bathroom?" Stony asked.

"It's over there," his father said, pointing out the front window. About fifty yards away was a small building, its outside lit with bulbs attached every five or so feet to a wire.

Stony turned his gaze from there to the cottage's back wall, discovering a fairly large circular window, about shoulder high, which looked out onto an enormous lake quietly absorbing moonlight. Under different circumstances this cabin would have provided a sanctuary for someone, a place to cast a fishing line and relax. The inside was sparse but comfortable. A picture of the White Mountains hung over one bed; over the other was a portrait of Abraham Lincoln. The beds were small but covered with soft red flannel spreads. The night had lowered the temperature to about sixty, and because Stony was wearing only a T-shirt, shorts, and sandals, he began to shiver again. His fever hadn't broken; the muscles in his arms and legs felt dense and heavy. All he wanted was to crawl under the covers.

"I'll be right back," his father said. When he returned he placed two bottles of water on the floor next to Stony's bed. "Just rest."

"That's not why I came."

"Just lie down. I have to do some checking. I'll be back in half an hour." He handed Stony his watch. "You can keep time."

It seemed pointless to argue, so Stony did as he was told.

His father pointed to the bottles of water before leaving. "Drink."

Alone, Stony crawled under the covers, fighting

to stay awake. He hovered between waking and sleep, where he could see what was going on in the room but also experience a freak show of hallucinations, as if projected from the back of his skull. There was John being gunned down on his grandmother's front lawn while hugging the bloody knife to his chest; there was the psychologist's sterile, book-lined study and the answerless questions sucking the air of the room; there he was tossing and turning, his sheets soaked as if he had wet himself. And every once in a while, in between these horrors, he'd be hiking a trail through the woods with his grandmother or helping her make Toll House cookies, licking the batter from a white plastic spatula. For what seemed like forever, he drifted like a dead leaf between these two worlds, until he sensed his father sitting next to him, placing a cool, wet washcloth on his forehead.

"What's happening?"

"I have these for you." He placed Stony's grandfather's ring into the palm of his left hand and closed it, then did the same to the other hand with Molly's bracelet.

"How did you get them?"

"It's not important. I still have to find Leopold."

"I want to go."

"You're not strong enough. I'd have to worry about you."

Stony tried to sit but couldn't.

"I won't be long. I know where he's camped." His father gently stroked Stony's cheek. "I love you," he said.

"I know," Stony answered.

There were other things Stony wanted to say, but he couldn't keep from drifting off.

When he awoke again, his fever had broken, his T-shirt was damp with sweat, and his breathing seemed easier. He felt the pressure of the ring and the bracelet in his hands, so he knew his father's appearance had been no dream. He slid the ring on, then opened a bottle of water and drank it in one gulp. He removed his T-shirt and tossed it toward the foot of the bed. Then he reached for the watch next to the remaining bottle of water. It was 1:15, which meant that he had been at the motel for close to two hours.

He opened the front door to find the Highlander missing and walked barefoot across pine needles to the restroom, where he washed up. Back in the cottage, he realized he didn't have another shirt, so he put on the damp one, its fabric clinging to his back. He slipped into his sandals and headed into the night, not knowing where he was going, except that his father's choice of motel meant that The Loon must be close by. He walked toward a route that was well traveled during the day but soundless at this hour. He was almost at the shoulder of the road when he heard someone say, "Where're you going so late?"

An old guy with a white brush cut and beard sat on a rocker that was perched on a cottage porch. He was smoking a pipe and wearing an old, thick white bathrobe, slightly opened to reveal two huge, muscular calves.

"I'm looking for a bar called The Loon."

"You old enough to drink?" the man said, smiling.

"I'm not going there to drink."

"Then I have to ask myself why you're heading there."

Stony didn't answer.

"Well, you're lucky I'm up. Insomnia. Even out here I can't sleep." He pointed inside the cottage. "The missus doesn't have that problem. If you listen, you can hear her snoring like a lumberjack." He started to laugh, then quieted himself, looking around, afraid he might wake up other lodgers. "Wait here," he said. He went into his cottage and returned with a white T-shirt he tossed to Stony. "You can't go around wearing that wet shirt or you'll get pneumonia."

"Thanks," Stony said, removing his old one and letting it fall to the ground. The new shirt fit surprisingly well.

"If you go about half a mile down the road," the man said, "you'll reach a dirt turnoff. About a quarter mile down that road is The Loon. It's not a place for you, though."

"I know."

"Do you mind me asking your name?"

"It's Stony."

"Stony, I don't know what you're doing, but be careful."

"I will," Stony said. He started to leave, then turned to say thanks again, but no one was there. He glanced around but saw only darkness and the chair slowly rocking back and forth.

Not a car passed him during the half-mile walk, the moon so bright it seemed to clear a path for him, the night's coolness giving him strength. He was eager to reach The Loon, to help his father if he could.

When he arrived at the dirt road, he bore left, straying into darkness. Out in front of him, in the distance, a faint neon sign glowed, and he jogged toward it. The Loon was a small rectangular building encased in cheap aluminum siding. Suddenly a large spotlight attached to a telephone pole came on, illuminating a dirt parking lot where Sally's Highlander was parked.

A man appeared on the front porch, holding a shotgun. "We're closed," he said.

"I'm looking for my father."

"I know who you're looking for."

The man wore new blue jeans, a black T-shirt, and shiny black cowboy boots with metal studs crawling up the sides. He was a big man: big arms and legs and a large stomach hanging over an oversize silver belt buckle. He pointed the barrel of the gun toward the ground. "Your father's crazy."

Stony almost laughed. "Where is he?"

"He busted up that fat hillbilly and scared everybody off."

When Stony kept walking closer, the man raised the gun and pointed it at him. "Where do you think you're going?"

"I have to see for myself."

"You won't be seeing anything if I blow your head off."

"Then that's what you'll have to do."

"You're a real pair of morons, you know?"

Stony nodded, continuing toward the door. When he reached it, the man stepped aside. He was right. The bar was empty. There were a few broken chairs off by a jukebox, and the mirror over the bar was shattered. On the floor next to the restroom was a mop in a bucket of water, and near the bucket, some blood. Stony peeked into the men's room, but it was empty, so he returned to the porch.

"When your father came through the door," the man said, "the fat one was right on him. I've had a lot of tough guys come through here, but I've never seen anyone put down a man so fast. But the fat one wouldn't give in. He got away for a moment. He threw a chair and smashed the mirror, but your old man broke him up pretty bad, and I said to myself, 'What's this about?' And then while the guy's barely conscious your old man grabs his hand and tries to yank his ring off, but it won't budge, so he breaks the guy's finger, and there's this ugly scream when the ring slides onto the floor." The man looked at the ring on Stony's finger and smiled, like it was all coming together. "Then he goes through the guy's pockets and comes out with a bracelet. He holds them up to everyone and says, 'These are mine,' and I nod, and so does everyone else. Just when he's about to leave, the fat one tries to get up, cursing and swearing, and your father kicks him in the head."

"Where was the skinny guy?"

"He wasn't there."

"What happened to the fat one?"

"We threw some water on him. I said I'd call the cops, but he said no, so some guys threw him into a pickup and took him to the hospital."

"Where's my father?"

"He went after the little guy."

"Where?"

"There's an old trail behind the bar that ends in the wilderness. Those yahoos have a camp up there."

"How long ago did he leave?"

"Maybe an hour ago."

Stony started toward the rear of the building.

"Good luck, son," the man said, shaking his head. "That skinny one's not right in the head."

The large light looming over the parking lot also shone down on the field behind the bar. Stony looked at the woods. About fifty yards away was a path, so he moved toward it, the high grass chafing his calves. As he got closer, the artificial light faded, replaced by faint moonlight. Finally he began his climb, the trail steepening within minutes. He waded through thickets of leaves and branches, grabbing on to whatever was in front of him. Black creatures hovered above, but they didn't scare him. It was the shudder behind a bush, the scratch of tiny, clawed feet, that made him pause.

Often the trail seemed to end, but then a finger of moonlight would point him in another direction. He had no idea where these paths went, but he wasn't concerned. It sometimes seemed as if the same forest that had coldly watched his family bound to trees was now guiding him. He climbed, losing track of time, moving confidently as if he had grown up in these woods. Every once in a while he would stop to look around, see some movement behind a tree, or hear the soothing hoot of an owl. He climbed higher and higher, the trees becoming shorter, patches of ground more spaced, until he felt granite beneath his feet and, looking up, he could see stars blinking on and off. When he reached the top, he stood on a rocky crag overlooking a large lake, moonlight revealing the shadows of homes and cottages. Some boats and dinghies were moored to man-made docks; others floated motionless as if glued to the lake's surface. He scanned the area, deciding what to do next, and then he heard a voice.

It was coming from his left, and when he turned, small puffs of smoke rose and dissolved into darkness. He dropped onto his hands and knees and crawled quietly toward the smoke, the smell of a campfire filling his nostrils. He could see a figure moving in the clearing. It was Leopold, and Stony was certain he had looked his way. He was crouched over a small fire, feeding it twigs.

To the right of him, his father sat, fastened with duct tape to the base of a tree.

Leopold removed a big hunting knife from behind his back and began to sharpen it against a stone, humming to himself. He came out of his crouch and knelt near Stony's father, rubbing the flat part of the blade against his father's cheek. Stony knew he had to make his move, but before he could get ready, Leopold stepped away, stationing himself on the edge of a cliff, surveying the lake below. When Stony crawled forward, hoping to reach his father, he loosened a stone—a sound that was barely audible but made Leopold tilt his head, so that the moonlight silhouetted his sunken cheeks. His ears seemed to enlarge and perk up, his nose elongating into a snout.

"I've been waiting for you, boy."

At the sound of Leopold's voice, Stony's father glanced worriedly around until he located Stony.

Stony didn't move. Either the moonlight or his lowly perspective made Leopold's figure loom large on top of the cliff. He appeared more animal than human now, clumping forward, waving the knife over his head while making agitated grunts. "It's time," he said, and with those words, Stony stood and faced him. There was nothing to be said. Instead, he began his attack by jogging, then picked up speed, the hard ground propelling him forward, until he sprung into the air, hoping to drop-kick Leopold and launch him off the cliff. Right before contact, he saw a bizarre smile break over Leopold's face, and he felt like he was gliding feet first through a ghost. If he hadn't seen Leopold soar into the night, he would've thought he had misjudged his leap.

Except Leopold was indeed airborne, his two arms flapping wildly, as if he might grow wings and fly away.

For what seemed like minutes, Stony hovered with him, wondering how far he himself would drop before his skull exploded on a boulder. Just as Stony was about to descend, he turned to see a large tree root sprouting from the top of the crag. He grabbed hold of it, the weight of his fall snapping the root taut, so that he now found himself dangling a few feet over the cliff's edge. Below him he heard a yell, then something like chanting, then finally a *thwack*, like the blade of guillotine on a wooden block.

And they threw him into the abyss,
   his toes pointing comically toward the heavens, as he hugged the knife to his chest, and this is what he saw:
   a boy treading black water in a river of water moccasins
   the hood ornament of the Taurus come to life and howling
   a sun-licked lizard sitting alone on a desert rock
   a dead body on the floor of a restroom at one in the morning
   centuries of human dust
   a bluebottle fly resting on the wrist of a little girl in Ohio
   a naked wall and heads with no faces
   that solitary star witnessing his descent, delivering him.

After Stony pulled himself to the top of the cliff and freed his father, they smothered the fire and found their way back to the Highlander. His father couldn't explain how he ended up taped to the tree. One minute he had Leopold pinned to the ground ("I could smell his breath"), the next, inexplicably, he was his prisoner ("It was like everything moved in slow motion"). Listening to his father, Stony was reminded of Sally's characterization of Leopold.

He and his father hiked down the trail and drove wearily back to the condo. Sally and Molly were sitting at the kitchen counter in pajamas, nervously drinking coffee. Sally hugged Stony's father, who did the same to Molly, not letting her go, as if afraid he wouldn't get her back. His father began to explain the night, but Sally placed a finger over his lips.

"Is it over?" she asked.

"Yes," his father said.

"You sure?"

"Yes."

Thinking about Abraham, Stony wondered if that was true.

"Then I don't want to know anything."

Stony could hardly stand. All he wanted was a quiet place to sleep. But before he left the kitchen, he dug into his pocket, bringing out Molly's bracelet. He gave it to her, kissing her on the cheek, then headed toward the bedroom. Molly followed, closing the door behind them. Stony sat on his bed, staring into predawn grayness. He thought about the last two days and about his grandmother and John, and he cried, Molly crying with him.

They all slept past noon. When Stony and his father awoke, they showered, worked on their wounds, and got dressed, his father wearing sandals to dry out the deep scratches he suffered while running barefoot down the mountain with Molly on his back. It didn't make any sense to stay. There was nothing for them there, and they knew they'd never return.

They spoke very little while packing, not wanting to slow down the process. Stony saw Molly's copy of *Tess of the D'Urbervilles* in a wastebasket and asked her if she wanted to bring it. "No," she said. "It's depressing."

As Stony carried the board games to the car, he noticed Sally and Molly standing near the bumper, lifting the cooler and positioning it behind the back seat, while his father arranged other belongings. They were preparing to retrieve the rest of their bags when a police car pulled up alongside of them. A huge man exited the driver's side.

Stony's father looked at Sally.

"I never made the call," she said.

Instead of a uniform, the officer wore a pair of tan khaki pants, black shiny wingtips, and a blue polo shirt. His head was large and round, topped with a blond brush cut that suggested he'd spent time in the service. All his weight and height seemed centered in his upper body; his legs, in contrast, were short, almost spindly. His arms were covered with blond hair, as were his hands, which seemed powerful. He had a crooked nose that took up half his face, and resting on its bridge was a pair of tortoiseshell glasses, making him appear professorial. There was nothing sinister about this cop, Stony thought. He approached Stony's father, holding out his hand, which Stony's father shook.

"Bud Philbrick," the cop said, completing the handshake. Then he scrutinized Molly, Sally, and Stony. Molly eased herself next to Sally, who held her close, a gesture the cop seemed to take note of.

"Arthur," Stony's father said.

"Yeah, I know. I asked at the office."

"Why would you do that?"

He sighed and stepped back. "I have a little problem, and it seems it's leading to you. Actually, it's not a little problem. One guy is dead and another is pretty messed up."

Stony looked at Molly and Sally, realizing that this was the first time they had heard details of the previous night.

"I don't see what that has to do with me," Stony's father said.

"Some people say otherwise."

Stony stepped next to his father while the cop reached into his back pocket. He pulled out two grainy mug shots, one of Leopold, the other of Abraham. "You ever seen these guys?"

His father scrutinized the photos, then handed them back. "No."

"Well, if you had a beef with them I wouldn't blame you. All reports suggest that the world would've been a better place if they'd been hit by a truck when they were four, especially this guy," he said, pointing to Leopold. "They've hurt a lot of people, but no one has ever been able to track them down. I called one cop in Louisiana who swears they're vampires." He waited for laughter that never arrived.

"Interesting," Stony's father said, "but we have to finish packing."

"Where're you going?"

"Home."

"Which is where?"

"Buffalo."

"Always wanted to take my kids to Niagara Falls."

"You should. It's worth it."

"Do you mind me asking what happened to your face and how you got that welt? And your boy seems to have a matching one." For a moment he fixed on Stony's father's bruised knuckles and scraped feet, but he didn't mention them.

Stony's father hesitated, and that's when Sally

spoke up. "I told him about New Hampshire mosquitoes and to go slow with the hiking, but he wouldn't listen."

The cop laughed and looked again at Stony's father. "Mind me asking where you and your boy were last night and in the early hours of the morning?"

"We were here, sleeping," Stony's father said.

"We can support that," Sally said, and Molly added, "My brother and I are sharing a room, so I know he was with me."

The cop nodded while scratching his chin. "Here's my problem. There's a real troublemaker in the hospital who's drinking his meals from a plastic straw, and the hospital calls me at two in the morning to say some guys in a pickup dropped him off. He won't say who attacked him, but it's a small town, and I hear that another guy driving a vehicle with your description did the beating. So I check around at different condos, showing photos of these two goons, and Laura down there in the office says this skinny one here, who's known as Leopold, was asking about you. Do you see the problem?"

"Yeah," Stony's father said, "But my daughter already told you where we were. Did this guy ask for me by name?"

"Not exactly. Laura said he described you."

"Well, there are a lot of guys who look like me."

The cop seemed in no hurry to leave.

Everyone was quiet until Stony said, "You said one guy was dead. What happened to him?"

"This is the strange part. There was a couple camping at the base of the mountain not far from Squam Lake. After they had breakfast, they went for a short hike, and found Leopold stuck in a tree like a broken kite. The branch was at least ten feet high and

I had to bring in a ladder to inspect him. His back was broken so badly his head nearly touched his heels. But the strangest part was that he had a big knife stuck in his heart and a crazy grin frozen on his face, like he enjoyed the fall." He looked at the cuts on Sally's knees. "Normally," he said, "if I were to describe something like that to a woman, she'd get upset."

"I think it's sad," Sally said, "but from what you said, maybe he had it coming."

"You're a tough lady," the cop said.

Stony's father walked over to Sally and kissed her on the forehead.

The cop probed the inside of his cheek with his tongue, then stuffed the photos into his back pocket. "Well, before you leave, do you mind giving me your license? I want to know where to contact you."

"No problem," Stony's father said, and he removed it from his wallet.

The cop took down some information, then handed back the license. "Mind if I talk to you and the boy alone for a minute?"

Stony's father hesitated, then asked Molly and Sally to wait inside.

After they left, the cop said, "I wanted to make a few points without the ladies present. First, the men who brought in Abraham said the guy who mangled him acted in self-defense." He waited unsuccessfully for Stony's father to respond, then continued. "Second, I want to stress what a badass this Leopold was. He's been linked to a number of gruesome murders all over the damn country."

"Like what?" Stony asked.

The cop sighed, as if deciding whether to describe them. "Let's just say they're not something one human would do to another, under any circumstances. I was in the first Iraq war, and one time we had the name of an insurgent whose specialty was beheading enemy soldiers, then sending the pictures to us. There were other crazies like him, and although we'd have their locations, we could never catch them, like they were protected by some diabolical force. Almost makes me sympathize with that cop in Louisiana."

"You mean you think Leopold was a vampire?" Stony said.

The cop laughed. "No, he was a lot scarier than a vampire."

"Why?"

"Because he was real, son."

"I'm not sure what your point is," Stony's father said.

"My point is that I have a job, and if you're involved in this, I've got a feeling you had your reasons, and, like I said, a lot can be hung on self-defense."

Stony remembered his father's comment, *They'd ask too many questions.*

"I don't know anything," his father said, "and my daughter . . ."

"Yeah, I heard her," the cop said, obviously disappointed.

There was an awkward silence, the cop scrutinizing Stony and his father, then checking out the condo window where Sally and Molly stood. "Damn," he said, "sometimes this job stinks."

Stony waited for the cop to escort them to the station, but instead he thanked Stony's father and returned to his cruiser. The engine turned over, but then the car door opened and the cop's left foot moved restlessly on the ground. The cop looked out at Stony and his father, shaking his head. Then he drew in his leg and backed out of the condo parking lot. After he left, Stony's father said, "Let's finish packing."

Before getting into the Highlander for the drive home, Stony looked around the condo site. It was a beautiful afternoon, cloudless and quiet. Most of the condo renters had left for the day. As they passed the pool, Stony took note of where he and Ruth had sat. He felt sad, but he knew the important thing was that they were going home. He had never thought he'd be content to sit in his room and admire the sunflowers, or take a jog around his neighborhood.

He was leaning his head against the window when his father said, "What now?" He pulled the car onto a dirt shoulder, and Stony turned, half expecting to spy the grille of the Taurus, driven by Leopold's ghost, but it was the cop again, who inched behind them and stepped out of his car. He approached the driver's side window, and Stony's father lowered it.

"Sorry to bother you again, but your left rear tire looks low. I'd say it's a slow leak."

"I didn't notice," Stony's father said.

"Mind if I show the boy?"

Stony's father hesitated, but Stony said, "No problem," and joined the cop, who walked to the rear of the Highlander and crouched down by the tire.

"This one here," he said. "You see it?"

Stony didn't but said yes. He was about to get back into the car when the cop led him a few feet off.

"What's your name?" the cop asked.

"Stony."

"I'm not sure what happened yesterday, Stony, but

will you do me a favor, since I don't think your father's listening to me?"

"Sure."

"When you get some quiet time with him, tell him I never want to see him around here again. I don't want to have to follow up on this. You hear what I'm saying?"

"I hear you," Stony said, walking back toward the car, then turning. "Thanks," he said, and the cop smiled.

Before driving off, Stony's father asked him what the cop had said.

"Nothing important."

"You sure?"

"Yeah."

"Okay," he said, heading toward the interstate, then past the trailers and gas stations and Burger Kings, past hills and small rivers that cut through them, past Concord with its gold-domed state capitol dwarfing old warehouses. Stony tried to relax but didn't feel safe until he saw the sign that read MASSACHUSETTS WELCOMES YOU.

No one said much as they drove down I-93 to I-495 and then to the Mass Pike. Molly slept most of the way, and his father played classical CDs Sally had packed. She was uncharacteristically fidgety, asking to stop every half hour, then disappearing into the ladies' room for a few minutes. His father kept asking if he could do anything, but she said no.

When they reached the New York State Thruway, they pulled into the first rest stop, about ten miles outside of Albany. Only Sally needed to go to the bathroom, and Molly was sleeping again. After Sally left, there was a moment of uncomfortable silence, broken when Stony's father asked if school started before or after Labor Day.

"Two days before," Stony said.

"Idiotic, huh, you just get back and then you have a break."

"Yeah," Stony said.

They sat quietly for five minutes, which quickly became ten.

Beginning to worry about Sally, they got out of the car and scanned the parking lot. Stony knew that Leopold was dead and that the Taurus was rotting in Jody's dusty lot, but he still half expected to see it parked nearby. His father obviously felt the same.

"I'm going to look for her," he said.

"I'm sure it's nothing, Dad. Let me go. I'd like to get a root beer anyway."

"Okay, but you have five minutes."

In McDonald's it didn't take Stony long to spot Sally. She was sitting in a corner booth staring out a window, not eating or drinking. When he sat across from her, she looked at him as if he were a stranger. Then a moment of recognition came over her face, and she began to cry, deep sobs that shook her whole body. Stony sat next to her and tried to hold her. At first she pushed him away, but then she held on to him tightly.

"He *was* evil, Stony," she said.

"I know."

"We did the right thing, didn't we?"

"Yes," he said, then hesitated for a moment. "You want me to get Dad?"

She slid away from him, trying to compose herself. "No, he loves me, but he wouldn't know what to say. I'm sorry, it's important to stay strong for Molly. Just go back and tell him I'm buying food, and that there's a long line."

"You sure you're okay?"

"Yeah." Then she grabbed Stony's hand. "He *is* dead, isn't he?"

"There's no reason for the cop to lie."

"No, I guess not."

When Stony returned to the car, he said what Sally had asked him to, and about five minutes later she came back carrying burgers and French fries and a few soft drinks.

"Since when do you eat that junk?" his father tried to joke.

Before he could say anything else, she kissed him on the cheek and said, "Just drive and don't wake Molly."

His father hesitated, then started the Highlander, directing it onto the Thruway. Sally passed a cheeseburger to Stony, which he bit into, surprised at how good it tasted.

EPILOGUE

On the Saturday of Columbus Day weekend, Stony and his father decided to play golf at South Park. The course was empty. The maples and oaks had shed most of their leaves, which made it hard to find balls, but he didn't care. He didn't even mind that they were playing the notorious third hole. There was no Al Capone on the green, and even if there were, Stony's father had not been himself since their return.

And that was good. He was regaining his sense of humor, but his jabs were good-natured, not mean-spirited. He and Stony had dealt with Leopold, so very little rocked their worlds. They were more concerned about Sally and Molly. No one ever spoke specifically about what had happened to Sally in New Hampshire. Somehow Sally and his father were dealing with Sally's side of it, mostly, it seemed, by focusing on Molly. Stony had wanted to tell his mother, but Molly swore him to secrecy ("She won't mean to, but she'll make it worse"), and Stony had decided to respect her wishes, trying to busy himself with school.

Right now he just wanted a little peace. Two months ago if he had felt that way he certainly wouldn't have golfed with his father, but lately they'd been getting along. Sometimes Stony worried about Abraham. He wondered if he might glance over his shoulder and see a broken-down truck bearing down on him. But at this moment, on this particular golf course, all he wanted was to hit an eight-iron three feet from the pin and one-putt for a birdie. He teed up and struck a nice high shot that headed for the center of the green until a breeze caught it and nudged it into a sand trap.

"Too bad," his father said, then added, "Just kidding."

"You better be," Stony said. "You're next."

His father was sitting on a yellow metal bench, pinching the shaft of a seven-iron between his knees. He was holding a piece of paper.

"What's that?" Stony asked.

"Sit for a second."

Stony joined him on the bench.

"Don't get mad, but this came to the house, and I opened it by mistake." He handed Stony the piece of paper. It was a letter from Ruth.

Stony unfolded the letter. *Dear Stony, I worked four weeks on that receptionist until she gave me this address. I hope it's the right one. I want to explain why I didn't tell you I was leaving. I wrote my phone number, email, and home address at the bottom. I hope you don't think I'm a jerk. Ruth.*

"So you read the whole thing?" Stony asked.

"Sorry," his father said, adding, "She does seem interesting."

"No offense, but it's hard to take advice from you about women."

"Touché," his father said.

"I didn't mean that to be nasty."

"I know."

Stony folded the letter and put it in his bag.

"You think you'll follow up on this?" his father asked.

"I don't know."

While Stony was zippering the pocket of his bag, his father teed up and hit a terrible duck hook about twenty feet into the pond, torpedoing a few decaying lily pads. He teed up again and did the same thing. "You're probably waiting for me to toss this club, aren't you?"

Stony smiled but didn't respond.

"Well, you're right," his father said, hurling the club end over end, like a baton, into the middle of the pond. They both laughed, then left the tee and dragged their carts through the wooded path leading to the green. "I can only change so much," his father said.

"I would have been disappointed if you hadn't tossed it," Stony said. "Now I have a juicy story to tell Mom."

"Ha!"

After they finished playing, they ate hot dogs at the clubhouse, and left the course a few hours before sunset.

"You want to come back to the house?" his father asked.

"No, I better go home."

"Sally made her famous zucchini bread," his father added. "Top it with vanilla ice cream and chocolate chips and you've got a pretty powerful dessert."

"You win," Stony said. His father's house was only a five-minute drive from the golf course and a five-minute walk from his mother's, so he knew he could have dessert, sit for a while, and be home before dark. He had a lot of schoolwork and wanted to do well this year to impress colleges.

As they approached the house, Stony's father unexpectedly brought the Grand Marquis to a halt.

"What's the matter?" Stony asked.

"I don't recognize that car," he said, motioning to a big white Ford Explorer, parked in the driveway. They inched closer until Stony could see its New Hampshire license plate, which made Stony's father pull quickly into the driveway. There were two little kids, a girl about three and a boy about five, running in the backyard, pushing around Sally's red exercise ball. Sally was standing with a young, attractive blond, and next to them with his back turned to the Highlander was a very large man. When Stony's father honked the horn, the man turned. It was the cop from New Hampshire, holding a beer in one hand, waving with the other.

"Damn," Stony's father said. "Just say as little as possible."

Stony nodded.

When they reached the backyard, the cop offered his hand and Stony's father shook it.

"I didn't think you'd remember me," the cop said. "We finally decided to make that Niagara Falls trip." He was wearing jeans, sneakers, and a hoodie with PLYMOUTH STATE COLLEGE stenciled on the front.

"So you decided to visit us?" his father asked.

The cop pointed toward his wife, who was talking to Sally. She waved at them and they reciprocated. "I told her we're kind of friends and I needed to talk to you."

Before his father could respond, Sally and the cop's wife joined them while the two children kicked and jumped on the ball.

The cop looked at Sally. "Your lady was nice enough to give me a beer and let the kids play for a while. She also makes a wicked zucchini bread." The cop's wife just smiled, and it was clear she was oblivious to the real reason for the visit, but then so was Stony.

"It looks like I should get some more," Sally said. "Why don't you and your wife relax while I make coffee." She pointed to a weathered picnic table about twenty feet away. "And I could use some help," she said to Stony and his father.

"Sounds good," the cop said, "but then I'd like to chat with your men and we'll be on our way."

Inside the house, Sally brewed a pot of coffee and asked Stony to slice some bread on a wooden cutting board.

"Why did you ask him to stay?" Stony's father asked.

"Because I don't want him to think we're hiding something."

"But we are," his father said, sighing. "Well, we might as well find out why he's here." So they waited until the coffee brewed, and then Stony and his father carried the zucchini bread and coffee outside and rested the trays on the picnic table.

After Sally poured everyone a coffee, the cop told Stony and his father that he wanted to show them something in the car, and they followed him to the Explorer. "I have some information for you," he said.

"Is it about Abraham?" Stony asked.

The cop laughed. "You don't have to worry about him."

"Why not?"

"When we located Leopold's camp, we discovered a gun, the one that killed a local hitchhiker, and Abraham's prints were all over it."

"Then what's the problem?" Stony asked.

"About a month ago there was a disturbance at The Loon, and when I got there, some stranger had knifed another guy. Almost killed him. There was something familiar about the stranger, and when I ran his prints, I discovered he was Leopold's brother. I should've known it when I saw him. He was scrawny and pointy and what I'd call dark. I was worried his mother might've given birth to a whole litter of these animals, but nothing came up. Still, guys like them appear and disappear like plagues."

"What happened to him?" Stony's father asked.

"With his record, the knifing will put him away for a long time, but I thought you should know."

"So you drove all the way to Buffalo to tell us?"

The cop smiled. "I told you we wanted to see Niagara Falls. To be honest, I tried to forget the whole thing, but I couldn't, so why not kill two birds with one stone."

"Thanks," Stony's father said.

"Is there anything we can do?" Stony added.

"No, it's probably over." The cop paused for a moment, then asked, "How's your sister?"

"Fine," Stony said.

"And your lady friend?"

"Everything's fine here," his father said.

The cop pointed toward the backyard. "You know, even though I'm a cop, I don't know what I'd do if anyone ever hurt my wife and little girl."

There was a brief silence, then Stony's father patted the cop on the back. "I appreciate the heads-up. Why don't you have more coffee and sit for a while."

"I'd like to," the cop said, "but I want to reach the Falls before dark."

Stony's father nodded, and they joined Sally and the cop's wife in the backyard.

After the cop left, Stony, his father, and Sally didn't discuss the unexpected visit. Stony finished his zucchini bread and coffee and walked home, saying he'd get his clubs later. Molly was waiting up for him, eating popcorn and watching a movie on TV. Since their trip, she had been more fearful, as if preparing for another tragedy, very much the way Stony had felt after his grandmother was murdered. But she was slowly regaining her sense of humor.

"A hot date?" she joked.

"If you call playing golf with Dad a hot date."

"I certainly wouldn't," she said, smiling.

He sat with her for a while, eating and staring mindlessly at the TV, until his desire to mention the cop became so overwhelming he had to say goodnight and go upstairs. In his bedroom, he lifted weights and tried unsuccessfully to distract himself by surfing the Internet. Then he opened Ruth's letter and tossed it onto his bed, her addresses staring up at him. He lay down and crossed his hands behind his neck, closing his eyes, though afraid to fall asleep, afraid he might wake to a new nightmare.

Early-evening sounds from the neighborhood invaded his room: children laughing, the *oooh, oooh* of a pigeon. Suddenly Leopold's face floated before him. At first he tried to ignore the perverse phantasm, but then he embraced it as you might an evil twin—Leopold's sunken black eyes, pointy chin, the thin, pale, shriveled lips curled into the permanent smile of a stripped skull. Stony wondered why he had needed to explain the actions of people like Leopold. Who cared why he had turned out so bad? All that mattered was that he had once existed and that he no longer did.

He rolled over and grabbed a pillow, pulling it toward his chest, feeling his body relax. Outside the children were laughing again, and he heard a mother's lilting voice calling them home.

Made in the USA
Charleston, SC
01 April 2014